## 'Which ones are yours?' Laird asked, beside Tammy. 'The kids, I mean.'

'Oh. Which ones? All of them!'

'All five?'

'Yes.' Was he turning pale? She wouldn't blame him. People often did.

'I somehow thought it was three,' he murmured.

'No, it's five.' She held up the correct number of fingers, just to drive the point home. 'Three four-year-olds—'

'Triplets!'

'You've turned pale.'

He really had.

'Five kids, including triplets,' she went on. 'That's why I need five ice-creams.'

'And you're on your own with them.'

Was he horrified or impressed? She couldn't tell.

He'd looked quickly down at his coffee, but somehow a memory had imprinted in his mind and he couldn't seem to let it go.

*I want her. In my bed. In my life.*

Bestselling romance author **Lilian Darcy** has written over seventy novels, for Silhouette Special Edition, Mills & Boon® Medical™ Romance and Silhouette Romance. She currently lives in Australia's capital city, Canberra, with her historian husband and their four children. When she is not writing or supporting her children's varied interests, Lilian likes to quilt, garden or cook. She also loves winter sports and travel. Lilian's career highlights include numerous appearances on romance bestseller lists, three nominations in the Romance Writers of America's prestigious RITA® Award, and translation into twenty different languages. Find out more about Lilian and her books or contact her at www.liliandarcy.com

Look out for a new book by Lilian Darcy next month!

A PROPOSAL WORTH WAITING FOR
is the next story in the fabulous mini-series
set in *Crocodile Creek*—available September 2008,
only in Medical™ Romance!

# THE CHILDREN'S DOCTOR AND THE SINGLE MUM

BY
LILIAN DARCY

MILLS & BOON®
*Pure reading pleasure*

First published in Great Britain 2008
Harlequin Mills & Boon Limited,
Eton House, 18-24 Paradise Road, Richmond, Surrey TW9 1SR

© Lilian Darcy 2008

ISBN: 978 0 263 19899 7

Set in Times Roman 10½ on 12¾ pt
15-0608-46771

Printed and bound in Great Britain
by Antony Rowe Ltd, Chippenham, Wiltshire

# THE CHILDREN'S DOCTOR AND THE SINGLE MUM

# CHAPTER ONE

'WE NEED another nurse,' Laird muttered.

He had one standing right beside him, checking the two resuscitaires, plugging in tubing for oxygen, laying out the plastic wrap that would help keep the twins warm once they'd been born. He could see the nurse mentally confirming that all the equipment on the resuscitaire trolleys was in place—laryngoscope, endotracheal tubes, Magill forceps—and she moved adroitly around the awkward positioning of various fixtures in the operating theatre.

She looked as if she knew exactly what she was doing.

All well and good, but one nurse wasn't enough. The scrub nurse and circulating nurse adding to the crowd in the operating theatre would be fully occupied on the surgical side. They weren't here for the babies themselves. This patient was about to have a Caesarean delivery.

Two paediatricians, one NICU nurse, two twenty-seven-weekers about to be born—it didn't add up, especially when the babies had stage three twin-to-twin transfusion syndrome. You really needed two medical people for each twin when they were going to be so fragile and small and ill and would need transfer to the NICU as soon as they were stabilised after birth. At least Sam Lutze was a good doctor, and the one neonatal nurse they did have seemed unfazed by the whole situation.

But she'd heard his muttered complaint.

'Sorry, but there's only me,' she said, calm and matter-of-fact, still checking her equipment. 'Someone's just gone off sick. We have a supernumerary and we're shifting things around, but for now… Yeah. You've got me.'

'It's not good enough,' he muttered again.

'I know. But we have a whole NICU full of sick prems. Someone's on the phone, seeing if there's anyone we can transfer to another hospital. We're doing our best.' She glanced over at the operating table, where their pregnant patient was about to be delivered, by Caesarean. 'Give Dr Lutze the recipient twin, if he's the strongest, and you and I can take care of the donor. Would that be the way to go?'

'We'll see how it pans out. I haven't met you before,' Laird said.

He couldn't help turning the statement into a challenge. It was one in the morning and Sam Lutze had called him in half an hour ago—Laird had only left the NICU two hours before that—when Fran Parry's obstetrician had decided her labour was unstoppable.

Laird had seen the latest scans and tests on the babies. They would have needed an emergency delivery within the next few days anyway, because the recipient twin had heart problems developing, while the donor twin just wasn't getting enough blood.

This woman…

What was her name? He discreetly checked her badge. Tammy Prunty. Was he reading that right?

She had better be *more* than competent at her job.

'No, you haven't met me,' she answered. 'But plenty of people at Royal Victoria NICU have. Dr Cathcart, Dr Leong, Dr Simpson. I was there for eight years, on and off, before I came here.'

*Here* being Yarra Hospital, several kilometres north-east of Melbourne's city centre, while Royal Victoria was closer in.

'Sorry, I wasn't pushing for your résumé.'

'Well, I can understand why you wanted it.' She unkinked a cable, switched something on. She had a comfortable figure—some people might call it plump, others voluptuous—but her movements were fast, deft and sure, and Laird had the grudging realisation that she seemed to know her way around the equipment better than he did.

'Don't tell me this is your first shift here, though, please!' He could hear all too well how crabby he sounded, but the prospect of staffing issues affecting a high-risk birth like this one always got to him.

'Nope,' she said. 'Second.'

'Oh, great!'

'But so far it's pretty similar to how we did things at RV. Everything's the same colour!'

Her calm good cheer soothed his irritation, and his impatience seemed to have affected her like water on a duck's back, thank goodness. Her disposable cap stuck out all around her head, like a cross between a pancake and a Madonna-blue halo, and her pale forehead was shiny above a pair of brilliant blue eyes. If she had hair, he couldn't see it.

They were ready for the babies now.

Or as ready as they'd ever be.

'Everything all right, Mrs Parry?' asked her obstetrician, Tim Wembley.

'I can't feel anything now.' Her voice sounded shaky, and her husband squeezed her hand and hissed out a tense breath. Both of them were understandably frightened and emotional. They were in their late twenties, which was starting to look young to Laird at thirty-four.

'That's the way we want it.'

'Good to go here,' the anaesthetist said.

'Not long now,' said one of the two theatre nurses, giving Mrs Parry's shoulder a pat. She was circulating, not scrubbed and sterile like her colleague. Both women had kept up a cheerful stream of reassurance, explanation and general chat as preparations for the Caesarean birth were completed.

'Dr Burchell, Dr Lutze, how are we over there?' Dr Wembley asked.

'We're good,' Laird answered, and Sam nodded, too.

Dr Wembley made the initial incision, working cleanly and with no fuss. When the babies were so fragile, they needed speed as well as a gentle touch. Being born could be a jarring process, even for a healthy baby at full term.

Laird watched, standing at the resuscitaire so that he'd be ready to work on the first baby as soon as he was freed from his mother's womb. The latest scan suggested this would be the smaller and frailer of the two—the so-called donor twin.

The Parrys understood the terminology by now. Laird had seen them in his office last week after it had become clear that the amniotic fluid reduction procedures weren't doing enough to help the babies.

They seemed like a pretty sensible couple. They knew

that roughly fifteen per cent of identical twins developed TTTS, with varying degrees of severity, and that it occurred when the webbing of blood vessels in the babies' shared placenta grew unevenly, creating a circulation system that favoured one twin at the expense of the other.

They'd asked him a whole lot of questions, which he'd done his best to answer. Unfortunately there'd been a couple of factors, including a badly positioned placenta, that had made laser surgery on the placental blood vessels a very risky option. This had meant that any treatment, including the amnio reductions and steroids to develop the twins' lungs, had only been an attempt to head off worsening problems, and had done nothing to deal with the underlying condition.

Scans showed that the donor twin—the one sending too much of his own blood into his brother—was undersized and passing too little urine, while the recipient twin's heart was enlarged and working way too hard as it attempted to deal with the excess fluid.

The Parrys already knew that their boys were lucky to have survived this far, and that one or both of the babies could still die.

'OK, here we go,' Tim said. 'Yes, this is the donor twin.'

'Adam,' said Chris Parry firmly. 'His name is Adam, for heaven's sake, not The Donor Twin.'

'Adam,' Tim echoed at once.

Parents were sensitive at a time like this. Laird had seen the racking emotions they went through over and over again, and it kept him humble. He wasn't a father himself. Not yet. Or not ever? Insufficient evidence to reach a conclusion on that one.

From what he regularly saw in the NICU, parenthood seemed to him like the dramatic, uncharted territory of an undiscovered island—alluring and frightening at the same time. He wondered if he'd have the same strength he saw over and over in the parents of ill babies.

'Nice. Look at that movement!' Tim said. It was feeble, but it was there. The baby was very pale. 'Hey, Adam, going to breathe for us?'

He wasn't.

No surprise.

He was blue and so small, well under a kilogram at a guess.

'What's our other one's name?' Tim was asking. After the dad's moment of anger and Tim's own carelessness, he'd recovered his sensitivity. These parents needed everyone to treat these tiny, fragile creatures as beloved human beings right from the start.

'Max,' Fran Parry said.

'Here comes Max.'

Laird didn't waste time waiting to see whether Adam's breathing would happen on its own. The NICU nurse took the tiny baby from the obstetrician's gloved hands into the dry, pre-warmed towel she had waiting, then laid him in the heated resuscitaire and folded the nest of plastic wrap over him, leaving his head and umbilical cord exposed. Laird decided he didn't need to suction the tiny nose and mouth. There was no evidence of meconium staining in the waters or blood visible at the baby's mouth.

In the resuscitaire, baby Adam seemed lost in a waste-land of white mattress. The nurse dried his head and covered it with blue tubular bandage, while Laird began the resuscitation process. He found a pulse at the umbilical artery—roughly sixty beats per minute—and said after a moment, 'We have a nice heartbeat.' He heard tearful sounds of relief from Fran Parry. 'We're going to get some oxygen into you right now, little guy.'

He found the heart-breakingly small premmie intubation equipment ready for him right at the moment he needed it and took it from the nurse. He had already forgotten her name. Something a bit odd and comical, which belied her wonderful competence.

'That's nice. That's good,' he said, just to reassure the parents.

OK, here we go, tube going down. Such a tiny distance, seven centimetres, and the tube was only 2.5 millimetres wide. Gently...gently...

The nurse—Plummy, he was going to have to call her for the moment, in his head, even though he knew it wasn't quite right—clamped and cut the cord, leaving several centimetres intact to allow umbilical line placement.

'Max is going to need some help here...' Tim was saying.

One of the theatre nurses took the recipient twin into a second warmed towel, laid him in the resuscitaire and wrapped him, while Sam Lutze checked his responsiveness on the Apgar scale. At a quick glance, Laird expected the one-minute score to come in at two or less. Adam's had squeaked to three, and he wanted it higher soon. His colour had begun to improve, some pink radiating outwards towards his little limbs.

'Swap,' Sam muttered to Laird, about Max. The one-syllable request acknowledged Laird's extra year of experience and his reputation for superhero skills at resuscitating the sickest babies. 'Look at him, it's his heart. And he's floppy, no reflex. Give me Adam, he's almost ready for transfer. Tammy, you'll stay with Max and Dr Burchell.'

She nodded, finished what she was doing at Adam's resuscitaire and switched straight to Max, wrapping the plastic, slipping the tubular bandage onto his tiny head with a couple of soft movements.

Laird devoted a critical few moments to repeating *Tammy, Tammy, Tammy,* over and over in his head, as he moved to the unresponsive baby. Max was a darker red than he should have been, filled with the excess of blood he'd innocently robbed from his much smaller brother. Thick blood, they often called it, because a baby's tiny liver couldn't process it and remove the waste. His heart had been struggling, and even without the TTTS the simple fact of prematurity could often present its own cardiac issues.

'Right, let's do this,' Laird muttered. He understood the junior doctor's reluctance. Max was going to be much harder.

He looked down at the baby, willing it to show some strength and fight, willing the parents' love to make a difference, to have some power over life and death. Later on it would. Premature babies responded wonderfully to the familiar voice of their mother or father, and to the right kind of touch. Now, though, it was more about medicine than hope.

'What's happening? Is he OK?' Chris Parry had sensed the increase of tension in the medical personnel, and he could probably see for himself that the second baby, although larger, wasn't looking as good as his twin.

His wife moaned. 'Max?' she said. 'Hang in there.

Mummy's here, and Daddy. We love you so much.' Her voice cracked and she couldn't speak any more.

'Is he going to be OK?' Chris asked again.

'We're going to do everything we can,' Laird said. Terrible words. Yet false promises were even worse, he considered. 'Tammy, start cardiac massage while I tube him.'

He hoped she'd sense when he needed her to get out of the way and that she wouldn't need to be talked through it.

'Adam's looking good,' Sam said, after a moment. 'I'm getting 85 bpm, his chest's moving. I'll get an umbilical line into him now. Then you can go for a ride, little man.'

Laird heard more sounds from the Parrys. Relief and anguish. Then from Tim a suspiciously calm 'All right, we're going to have to pack this. Do we have some blood, Helen?'

Mrs Parry had begun to bleed too much, a reasonably common side effect following the procedures she'd had over the past few weeks to reduce her amniotic fluid. 'What's happening? What's going on now?' Chris demanded, distraught. Like his wife, he had fair, freckled colouring, which made him look very pale under the harsh lights. Fran's lips were white.

Laird couldn't spare a thought for them right now. Max needed him too much, needed the tube, needed the massage, needed treatment for that thick blood and some relief for his heart as soon as they had him stable.

At every moment, the Tammy nurse was there. Hands in the right place. Voice pitched low enough to soothe the baby but loud enough for Laird to hear. Fingers nimble and delicate. No unguarded exclamations of doom to scare the stricken parents. Laird spared her a glance and managed a muttered 'Thanks.' She nodded, and there was this odd little moment that he didn't understand. More than mere relief at being paired with a competent colleague. More like…recognition?

He didn't have time to think about it now.

Chris had tears streaming down his cheeks. Fran was pressing her dry lips numbly together and clamping a death-like grip on her husband's hand.

'Come on, darling,' Tammy cooed to the baby. Her fingers seemed to flutter against his miniature sternum, and her voice was delicious, soft and musical and honey sweet. 'Come on, sweetheart, let's see what a big strong boy you are. Let's try really hard…'

'OK, he's tubed,' Laird finally said. Like Tammy, he'd almost been holding his breath. He saw her nod and look of relief. She cared. 'Heart rate's coming up. Not counting chickens…' he added quietly.

She understood. 'Want the umbilical line?'

'Can you? I'll give a first dose of adrenalin via the ETT, but let's have that UVC.'

She got the line in with incredible speed and dexterity and he delivered a carefully calculated dose of adrenalin through the endotracheal tube. Next, Tammy nested the baby in a rolled and warmed towel and adjusted the radiant heat setting.

Time had passed, ceased to have meaning. All of this took longer than a non-medical person would expect.

'Let's move him now,' Laird murmured. 'We need to get him stable and quiet, get him under bili lights to get his blood sorted out, and this is torture for the parents.'

'I know.'

He raised his voice a little, and told them, 'We're ready to move him to the NICU now.'

'Can Chris go with you?' Fran asked feebly. Tim was still packing her uterus to stop the haemorrhaging and she looked very pale and weak, alert through sheer force of will and a desperate need to know how her babies were doing.

'Chris, it's better if you stay here until Fran's in Recovery,' Laird said. 'Then you should be able to come and see both babies and let her know how they are.'

It would be an enormously stressful time for her, he knew. This first hour. The first day. The first week. No guarantees, yet, as to if or when she'd be taking her babies home—her own process of recovery from the stressful pregnancy, the surgery and blood loss almost an afterthought.

The journey to the NICU was short, and there was an incubator already set up for Max at thirty-six degrees Celsius and eighty-five percent humidity. Little Adam had a nurse working over him, checking his temperature, setting up more lines and monitors, applying a pre-warmed soothing and moisturising ointment to his skin.

They moved Max from the resuscitaire into a second incubator, weighed him in at 830 grams, took his temperature and began to set up and secure his lines. The Tammy nurse with the beautiful voice went looking for a bili light and Laird put in an order for blood for Adam, who weighed just 580 grams. Sam was called to the other end of the room to assess one of his patients whose oxygen saturation levels had fallen.

'Just need to tell you, Tammy, I'm going home, taking a break,' announced a mother some minutes later, coming over to her after she'd returned with the phototherapy equipment. The woman spoke too loudly and seemed not to notice tiny Max in his humidicrib or that Tammy was now busy making notes in the baby's brand-new chart. Again, Laird had lost track of time, except as it related to observing Max.

Tammy looked up from her notes. 'That's sensible, Mrs Shergold.' She took the woman's arm and led her gently away from Max. She spoke quietly. 'You were only discharged this morning, weren't you?'

'I know. I wanted to stay another couple of days, but no go. It's just wrong, isn't it? It's the insurance companies, and the government. Do they have any idea?' She still spoke too loudly, hadn't picked up on the soft cue given by Tammy's lowered voice.

Laird caught an angry glance in the woman's direction from an exhausted-looking blonde mother in a nightgown and slippers, who was bending over her own baby's humidicrib.

*One* of her own babies' humidicribs, he corrected mentally as he took in who she was. She'd had IVF triplets. Twenty-nine-weekers. Another Caesarean delivery. Five days old. All three babies were very, very fragile and ill. The mother moved gingerly, her incision still fresh and sore, making way for a nurse who was due to give another session of clustered observations and medication.

'How's your baby doing?' Tammy asked the loud woman, still pitching her voice low.

Again the woman ignored the cue regarding her own volume. 'Oh, she's great, she's so beautiful! It's so hard to see her like this!' She burst into noisy tears. 'But she's coming off the ventilator tomorrow!'

Tammy led her farther away towards the corridor. The mother of triplets checked her babies' oxygen saturation levels on the monitor. 'Look, they've dropped,' she said, low and angry, to the babies' nurse. Clearly she blamed the disruptive and self-absorbed presence of the other mother, and quite possibly she was right.

When Tammy came back, she patted the triplet mum—Alison Vitelli—on the shoulder and asked, 'How's Riley?'

'Oh…the same, Dr Lutze says.' She didn't look as if she'd brushed her hair that day, and even her skin looked tired. 'Tammy, can you, please, please, keep that horrible woman away from here?'

'Well, she has a sick baby of her own.'

'A thirty-two-weeker!' Mrs Vitelli said angrily. 'She keeps crowing about Rachelle's progress, and how she'll be graduating out of here in a day or two to the special care unit, as if we all care. As if any of us care! We would care, if she was nicer. But hasn't she noticed how ill the rest of our babies are? I hope Rachelle does get better fast, because if her horrible mother is around here much longer…' She trailed off into silent, desperate sobs, and Tammy hugged her and soothed her, stroking her back below the unbrushed tangle of blonde hair.

'I know, I know,' she murmured. 'Try to tune her out, if you can. She's not important. People can be insensitive sometimes.'

'Just her,' Mrs Vitelli sobbed. 'I hate her! I really hate her! She's appalling. And I'm going home tomorrow, and I don't want to leave my babies…'

Tammy looked over Mrs Vitelli's shoulder and caught Laird's eye. She was still patting the woman's back and making low, soothing sounds of agreement, caring—he thought—more than she really should. He read the questions in her face. *Is this OK? Do you need me? How is Max?*

He made a gesture that said, *Stay with her till she's feeling better*, and Tammy nodded. 'How about you go back to your room and get some sleep now, before morning, Alison?' she said gently. 'Your babies don't need you to get this tired…'

It took Tammy several minutes to soothe Mrs Vitelli's sobs away and persuade her that sleep was the sensible thing, then she came back to Max and noted the next set of figures in his chart. 'Oxygen saturation is up,' she said.

'Hovering at 93 per cent,' Laird answered. '$CO_2$ is within range. I changed the settings a little, as you can see. So far he's handling the sedation. And he peed.'

'Wonderful! Adam hasn't…?'

'No, not yet.'

'Let's hope.' She cast a practised eye over the monitors, checking the relationship between the various settings. Any time she came near the babies, something changed in the way she moved. She became even gentler, even calmer—but it was more than that. Laird couldn't put his finger on it.

'You must have managed a fair bit of practice with some of this stuff over at Royal Victoria,' he said, curious to know just how lucky he might come to consider himself, professionally, that she belonged to Yarra Hospital now instead.

Beneath the blue halo of her cap, she grinned. 'They even let us loose on real babies sometimes.'

Laird still hadn't seen her hair. He had a horrible feeling he might not recognise her if he saw her in another part of the hospital, garbed in street clothes. Her colouring and features were average—Scottish skin, those amazing blue eyes, pretty-ish, from what he could tell, in a nursy kind of way. In his experience, women didn't go into nursing if they looked like they could be models—which was probably to the benefit of both professions.

Keeping his voice low, he asked, 'Why did you make the move?' He waited almost smugly for some line about the fantastic reputation of the NICU at Yarra. He'd felt fortunate to win a position here himself, and intended to bring the profile of the place even higher as he worked his way into a more senior role.

'It cuts seventeen minutes off my commute,' she answered at once, without smiling.

He smiled in response, though, and conceded, 'Question too personal for this time of night? OK. That's fine.'

'No, I'm serious.'

'You changed hospitals to cut seventeen minutes off your commute?'

'Seventeen minutes each way, four or five days a week, that's more than two hours. You can get a lot done in two hours.'

'I suppose you can. A couple of routine Caesareans, a good session at the gym, a DVD with a glass of wine.'

'The vacuuming,' she retorted. 'Two casseroles ready to freeze. Three parent-teacher conferences and a stock-up at the supermarket. Nuclear disarmament, that could be doable in two hours, I reckon, if I really pushed. At least, it sounds easier to my ears than getting the garden in shape. And then there's...*sleep*.' She uttered the word with longing.

He laughed. 'Those things, too.' He belatedly registered the fact that she seemed to have three children and realised he was in the presence of a genuine dynamo—one of those women who'd explored the wild island of parenthood and survived intact.

Then one of Max's monitor alarms went off, they both took it as a signal to get back to work, and he didn't think anything more about her for the rest of the night.

'Mum-mmee-ee!' All three triplets cannoned into Tammy within three seconds of her arrival in the kitchen via the back door. Having braced herself for the onslaught, she withstood it, bent down, hugged three four-year-old bodies—two sturdy, one still a little smaller than his sisters, as he probably would be until puberty.

'Leave Mummy alone, guys,' said Tammy's mother, who wasn't yet dressed, just wrapped in a towelling robe over a floaty nightgown and boat-like slippers. What time had the kids woken her up? The crack of dawn, as usual?

'It's fine,' Tammy told her. 'I have seventeen extra minutes now, remember? Nineteen, if I get a really good run and hit all the green lights.' She'd resisted leaving Royal Victoria for a long time, reluctant to lose the familiarity and the friendships, but the shorter commute had won out in the end.

'Well, spend eight of them with the kids and the other nine on extra sleep,' her mother drawled, as if she shared Dr Laird Burchell's opinion of the value of seventeen minutes. She should know better! 'You're back there at three, aren't you?'

'And an eight-till-eight on Saturday. But then I'm off until Tuesday night.' Tammy had been very firm with the hospital about not working daytime shifts on weekends.

Mum could come in from her garden flat at the back of

the house and handle the kids when they were at school and
pre-school during the day, or when they were asleep at
night, but it wasn't fair to ask her to babysit regularly on
weekends in daylight hours when they were all home or
shuttling around to soccer and swimming.

Not when there were five of them.

Not when the army had transferred Tom to Darwin two
years ago, giving him the excuse he'd been looking for, for
the past five years, to cut himself off from their lives. He
hadn't seen the kids since the Christmas before last.

The money he sent as part of their divorce settlement
was *just* regular enough and *just* generous enough to keep
Tammy from taking him to court, but was nowhere near
enough to cover what five children and a hefty mortgage
really cost. With a generous gift from Mum, she'd
managed to buy out his share of the house, but had
nothing in savings now. They lived from pay cheque to
pay cheque.

So, yes, physically, Tom had been gone from their day-
to-day lives for two years. Emotionally, he had been absent
since the day he and Tammy had found out that her planned
third pregnancy was going to deliver three babies instead
of one, following the births of Sarah and Lachlan who had
then been aged four and two.

She and Tom had been formally divorced for three years.

Sometimes she still found it hard to understand how he
could have done it, how his panic at the prospect of triplets
could have brought such an ugly, self-absorbed side of
him to the surface. How much had he simply been looking
for a good excuse to bail out? How long would their
marriage have survived even without the triplets?

Don't go there, Tammy, she told herself. Not when you're this tired.

She'd been angry and deeply wounded by his betrayal for a long time. Mostly, she was over it now. Sometimes, though, on a bad day—on the way home from work at close to midnight or when the money was stretched so tight she expected something to snap—yes, she took a backward step and got angry again. It was like what parents said about the NICU. A roller-coaster ride. Three steps forward, two steps back.

'How was work, anyway? An easy night, I hope,' Mum asked.

'I wouldn't recognise an easy night in the NICU if it jumped up and bit me. But we managed to get two fragile little twins through their first six hours. I'll have my fingers crossed for them all day.'

'You won't,' Mum retorted. 'Because you'll be asleep.'

'True.' She yawned, aching for her bed the way some women ached for a lover.

Her mother decreed, 'Someone else can cross their fingers.'

'Sounds good.' She thought about Dr Burchell again. He might cross his. He seemed to care. Well, neonatology wasn't a field you went into if you didn't.

She had a sudden flashback to the time he and she had spent getting Max stable in the delivery room, bending their heads over the little boy, reaching past each other. He'd looked at the baby with a kind of intensity that had almost generated heat, and there hadn't been a moment where she could have doubted his skill or his attitude.

'Going to eat something before you sleep?' Mum asked.

'Nah. Not hungry.'

'You'll fade away to a shadow.'

'Yeah, right!' She patted her backside, principal storage facility for the extra kilos she'd packed on over the past few years. They were her best friends, those kilos. They wouldn't let her down. They would be there for her through life's ups and downs, solid and real, keeping her very, very safe. After all, what man would even think of getting close to a woman with five kids, no money and this much padding on her frame?

*I am not on the market*, the extra kilos said on her behalf, which meant she could focus on what really counted.

Making ends meet.

Being a good mother.

Getting enough sleep.

'I'll just make their lunches, then head upstairs.' She yawned, wondering what was still in stock on a Friday, the day before shopping day. Any biscuits left? Any fruit? Her stomach rebelled. She was way too tired to think about food.

'I've already done their lunches.'

That brought her close to tears. 'Oh, lord, Mum, what would I do without you?' They hugged each other, and Tammy could almost feel through Mum's body heat all the things she wasn't letting herself say about Tom.

Ten minutes later, with the alarm set for two-twenty that afternoon when a couple of weeks ago she'd had to set it for two o'clock, she sank into sleep.

# CHAPTER TWO

LAIRD WAS late getting to Tarsha's elegant townhouse in Kew to pick her up for their Friday night date.

Little Adam Parry had given them a scare this evening. Alarms going off. The wrong numbers rising or dropping on his monitors. Laird had had to spend an extra twenty minutes at the hospital on his way to his evening out, adjusting medication doses and ventilator settings, and answering several anguished questions from the parents.

Chris and Fran Parry had wanted the kind of certainty that he couldn't truthfully give them, and yet it would be disastrous if they sank into hopelessness. There were some parents who detached themselves from their baby emotionally if they thought it wasn't going to live, in a desperate kind of defence mechanism that they didn't consciously choose. But premature babies needed their parents. The sound of a mother's soothing voice could raise their oxygen saturation when it dropped in the presence of medical staff. Even when they were so tiny, they seemed to know when they were loved, and to respond.

He'd found himself looking for the Tammy nurse several times during his visit to the unit, as if she might have been able to bail him out with the Parrys, phrase things better than he could himself, help the couple find the right balance between love and hope and realism. Someone had mentioned her name, but apparently she was on her break and he'd left again before she returned.

Tarsha greeted him at her townhouse door in a cloud of expensive perfume, her model's figure immaculately clad and her flawless face beautifully made up as always, to make the most of her dark hair and brown eyes, but when he leaned forward to kiss her—cheek or mouth, he hadn't made up his mind—she pulled back and he saw that she was tense.

'What's up?' he asked her.

'Nothing…'

'Come on, Tarsh.'

'We'll talk about it at the restaurant.'

'We'll talk about it *now*.'

'Must we?'

'Yes. Have some pity for a weary man with fraying patience and don't play games.'

'All right…all right.' She sighed, and tucked in the corners of her mouth. 'You win.'

They'd known each other for a long time as their parents moved in the same well-heeled social circles and were friends. They had first gone out together more than twelve years ago while Laird had been a medical student, but then Tarsha had chosen the lure of modelling in Europe and they'd called it quits, with no hard feelings on either side. There'd always been something missing at heart.

'What is it, Laird?' Tarsha had said once, back then. 'It's like a hundred-dollar bill that you know is a forgery. It looks right, but something still tells you it's not.'

Maybe they just hadn't been ready at that point. Too young. Too ambitious. Not enough time for each other.

A few months ago, after a successful modelling career, followed by several years spent working in the field of public relations in Paris, Tarsha had come home without the intended notch of a fabulous marriage on her belt. She was now in the process of starting her own modelling agency in Melbourne, which involved a lot of networking and schmoozing, as well as getting the right faces and bodies in her stable.

Laird had the vague idea that something had turned sour for Tarsha in Europe—that she was running away from a professional or personal disaster—but so far she hadn't shared the details with him.

Some conniving between their two mothers several weeks ago had led to a choreographed cocktail party encounter —'You remember Laird, don't you, darling?'— and Laird had understood at once that he was supposed to pick up again with Tarsha…no, not quite where they'd left off. People changed in twelve years.

Close, though.

The prospect had appealed on some levels. There was something out there that he hadn't found yet—a core of happiness and stability that he saw in the best couples and that he wanted in his own life. Maybe this time with Tarsha, the timing would be right. It was hard to question a relationship that was so perfect on paper, especially when it had been so neatly deposited in his lap, gift-wrapped.

Before Tarsha's timely return to southern shores, and after a long and carefully selected series of suitable girl-friends, his mother had asked him in exasperation a couple of times, 'What are you looking for in a woman, Laird, that you haven't managed to find yet?'

'Is that a rhetorical question?'

'You're thirty-four!'

He hadn't attempted to give her a list of attributes, but had half-heartedly tried to come up with a private one for himself.

He couldn't.

Somebody different. A breath of fresh air.

Not exactly a precise description.

'I'll know it when I see it,' he had predicted to his mother, confident and a bit grumpy.

Suddenly, looking at Tarsha's set face, he realised that this relationship…this woman…wasn't it.

It turned out she knew it as well as he did.

'I've realised this isn't working, Laird,' she said. 'Us, I mean.' And when he was silent for a fraction of a second too long, she went on quickly, 'To use the old cliché, it's not you, it's me. Something happened in Europe. A man. I'm not ready, and you're not the right person. And you know it, don't you?' She gave him a narrow-eyed look, and then she laughed. 'Hell, you really do know it! I can see the relief in your eyes.'

He couldn't deny it. 'I like you very much, Tarsha.'

'And I like you.' But she hadn't yet relaxed. He wanted to put an arm around her purely for reassurance, didn't quite know why she was turning this into a problem, as it was clear neither of them had any regrets.

'So we're fine, aren't we?' he said gently. 'We've both realised. We both feel the same. We can forget dinner tonight, if you want.'

'No, you see, that's what I don't want.' She took a deep breath, gave a big, fake smile.

'I'm sorry?'

'The it's-not-you-it's-me thing was the easy part.'

'Pretend I'm not getting this, and explain.'

'Laird...look at me!' Were those tears she was blinking back? 'I'm not the kind of woman who goes out with her single women friends in a big group and doesn't care what anybody thinks. I want to be honest with you about this. Pathetic and needy, but honest. Can we still go out sometimes? Would you be the man on my arm when I need one? I'm setting up this agency, I have to look good, I have to be seen. That's all. I just need a part-time, very presentable man.'

She spread her hands, did that dazzling pretend smile again and he realised how vulnerable she was beneath the glamorous façade, thanks to this unknown man in Europe. He realised, too, how little value beauty could have to a woman in the wrong circumstances.

He told her sincerely, 'Sure, Tarsh, I can be your presentable man, occasionally. I don't see anything getting in the way.'

She nodded and kissed him quickly, not on the mouth, but close. 'Good. And if I haven't made this clear, sex is not included in the deal. I—I...' Still smiling, she blinked back more tears. 'Somehow—and, please, don't grill me on the details here—I turn out to be a lot more monogamous than I would have thought.'

And that was that.

At the restaurant Laird and Tarsha had to wait for their table, wait for the menu, wait to be asked for their order and then wait for it to arrive. Neither of them seemed to have much to say, having dealt with the principal matter of interest between them before they had even left her house.

Laird fought hunger, irritability and fatigue, and Tarsha finally appealed to him, 'Talk to me, Laird! Talk shop, if you want, rather than the two of us sitting here like this. It's what you're thinking about, isn't it?'

He admitted that it was. 'We have some very fragile babies in the unit at the moment. Delivered two of them last night, and we were short-staffed. Fortunately, we had a terrific new nurse. I don't think both babies would have made it out of the delivery suite without her. She was fabulous. Down-to-earth, unflappable, knew her stuff inside out.'

'Pretty?'

He thought for a moment, and remembered the shiny forehead and the unflattering angle of Tammy Prunty's disposable cap. 'Um, I don't think so. Not really.'

Tarsha's attention had wandered. 'Is this ours?' she murmured, watching a waiter with laden hands. 'No, it's not…'

Laird was still thinking about the fact that he'd just completely slammed the Tammy nurse in the looks department. He felt guilty and impatient with himself, which was ridiculous. 'Although I never saw her hair,' he said, wondering about it, remembering the blue of her eyes. 'I have an idea she'll be a redhead, though.'

'She *will* be?'

'When I see her without her cap.' He looked forward to resolving the question, for some reason.

Tarsha fixed him with a suspicious look that he didn't understand, and then their waiter came towards them at last.

* * *

'And it was green, and we thought, Good grief, what is this? I mean, neon green newborn milk curds. The intern went pale. Poor thing, it was his second day, he didn't have a clue. He's about to call the senior surgeon, who has *no* patience with new doctors.'

'None of them do!'

'And then we see an empty bottle on the floor, and it's not from the baby at all. His big brother had one of those athletic power drinks, those "-ade" ones, and he'd spilled some of it, right on top of where the baby had spat up, only he was too scared to say.'

There was a chorus of laughter, cutting off a little too quickly when the three women in the staff break room saw Laird.

Red, he thought.

Just as he'd suspected from her colouring. Tammy Prunty had a magnificent head of gleaming bright carroty, goldy, coppery, autumn-leafy hair with a natural, untamed wave that would absolutely require full confinement beneath a cap any time she was anywhere near surgery or vulnerable babies. No wonder he hadn't been able to glimpse it before.

She smiled at him, her face receptive, friendly and polite and her blue eyes still alive from her recent laughter. The eyes and the hair went together like burnished gold and lapis lazuli in a piece of Ancient Egyptian jewellery, and the smile was so warm and dazzling it rendered him temporarily without words.

He'd heard her voice, coming past the break room, and had decided to settle the question of her hair now, at the first opportunity, because it had been nagging at him after he and Tarsha had talked about it on Friday night. He hadn't expected to feel so awkward, standing in the break room doorway the following evening.

The three nurses waited for him to get to the point. What did he want them to do? Which of them did he want to yell at? What information was he seeking?

'Just checking something,' he murmured vaguely, and left again, unsettled.

He heard the chorus of female voices pick up before he reached the end of the corridor, and had a weird desire to go back, make himself a coffee and sit down to join in. He would sit across the table from Tammy, so he could try to work out just what it was that he found so appealing about her colouring when he hadn't thought her pretty before.

He resisted the impulse, squared his shoulders and got on with his life instead.

Back in the NICU, the Parry babies had lived through their first two days but still had a long way to go. No one was even thinking about discharge yet. And they had a new thirty-four-weeker, Cameron Thornton, delivered via Caesarean and now five days old.

He wasn't on a ventilator and was only here because he had a bright, vocal mother and because, despite the recent scarcity of beds, several babies had been upgraded, transferred or discharged since Thursday night so the NICU now had two places spare, while the high dependency unit and special care unit were overflowing.

'Something's not right,' the mother had been saying since a few hours after his birth, even though he was breathing and feeding and doing all the right things.

Many six-week prems required almost no medical intervention and could be discharged within days of birth. According to Mrs Thornton's dates, he should have been a thirty-six weeker but a range of well-defined developmental signs had led Dr Lutze, who'd been on hand at the birth, to lower the estimate to thirty-four weeks or even a few days less, and Mrs Thornton had admitted she might have got it wrong.

She didn't think she was wrong about her current sense of concern, however. 'He's my sixth child. A mother knows.'

And sometimes they did.

This mother, Laird wasn't sure about. The baby's dad, Alan Thornton, was a senior administrator in the Faculty of Medicine at Yarra University, which meant he had contacts and influence. The mother was supposed to go home tomorrow, and Laird wondered if, with such a large family awaiting her attention, she simply wanted another night alone with her baby, or more time to rest in the relatively cushy environment of her private hospital room.

She did seem genuinely anxious, however. She was hovering over the baby, watching every change in his breathing and in the numbers on his monitor. Alison Vitelli, the mother of the triplets born at twenty-nine weeks, gave her a couple of the same resentful looks she'd given the other mother in here on Thursday night.

It had begun to look as if one of Alison's babies wouldn't make it, although two of them were doing better now. The smallest at birth, little Riley, had a whole raft of cascading problems, including a serious bleed in the brain, and Alison was again finding it very hard to deal with a mother whose child seemed barely unwell at all.

This mother wasn't making a song and dance to earn Mrs Vitelli's disapproval, however. She sat quietly, very sensitive to the presence of other babies and parents around her.

'How's he doing, Mrs Thornton?' Laird asked her in a murmur.

'His temp is up—37.8 degrees.'

A tiny bit higher than normal, Laird registered, but a baby wasn't considered febrile until its temp went over 38. The little guy still had nasal oxygen prongs for several hours each day, but the rate had been turned right down. They'd increased his periods of weaning from the machine, and he should be safely on room air by tomorrow.

Laird felt somewhat annoyed with Melanie Thornton, even though he was possibly being unfair. 'A mother knows', plus a tiny elevation in temperature, on top of a low-risk level of prematurity. How could he justify a barrage of expensive or time-consuming tests on that basis? If the NICU hadn't been, briefly and unusually, the only place with a spare newborn bed, this baby wouldn't even be here at all.

'I think you're worrying too much,' he told her, managing to keep his voice gentle.

'He's my sixth child.'

'So you've said.'

'Don't you think I'd be worrying *less* after five babies?'

'Not if this is your first premmie. Of course it must feel different. He's smaller, his skin is thinner, his lungs are less developed, he tires more easily when he tries to feed, all sorts of things.'

'It's more than that,' she insisted. 'I just feel it.'

Tammy Prunty was back from her break and ready to swap places with Eleanor Liu, who'd briefly taken over care of the Parry twins. Laird experienced an exaggerated wash of relief when he saw her coming, her hair now back under the unflattering blue pancake of its cap, which as usual made the smooth skin of her forehead look too shiny and white. He intercepted her before she reached Eleanor, and lowered his voice.

'Listen, can you do something about the Thornton baby? Or the Thornton mum, really. She's bugging me with her earth-mother intuition, and I'm really not convinced anything is wrong.'

'Do something?' She made a face. Her mouth went crooked, which drew Laird's attention to a detail he hadn't noticed until now. She had the most beautifully shaped lips, soft and smooth and pink.

'Work out what's going on,' he said, as if it should be easy.

'Work it out? Just like that?' It was cheerful, just a tiny bit reproachful, as if he was presuming too much on very slight acquaintance, which he probably was. Just because they'd saved a life or two together a couple of days ago. How dared he make the assumption that she was that good at her job? said the twinkling blue eyes.

'I'll buy you coffee,' he said, surprising both of them, then added, to make it clear he'd been joking…half, anyway, 'Provided your diagnosis is correct, obviously.'

She kept it light, too. 'Deal! Coffee it is. And not bad coffee in a paper cup either, or it doesn't count. The proper stuff, in good china. You want me to diagnose via the laying on of hands? Or are we more into reading animal entrails at this hospital?'

'You're good with that?'

'I was seconded to the animal entrail department at Royal Victoria for a whole week.'

'Mmm, and I've heard their facilities are state of the art.'

'I'll do what I can, Dr Burchell, but, you know, apparently this hospital does do *tests* occasionally.' Her blue eyes were still teasing him, inviting him to share the joke. 'You could order a couple of those.'

OK, time to reassert his authority before this whole exchange got out of hand. 'I'll do that,' he said, 'when I've narrowed down the options. That's what I need you for.'

Great, Tammy thought. What have I just promised? And why did I keep smirking at him like that, and trying to make him laugh?

Because you wanted to see him smile, said a sneaky little voice inside her.

He'd smiled at her just now from the doorway of the break room, and she'd smiled back, as if they knew each other quite well. She hadn't noticed in the delivery suite on Thursday night how good-looking he was—not exactly male model material, because he was too seasoned for that and he frowned too much, she could tell from the lines that had begun to etch into his forehead, but definitely at the more attractive end of the male doctor spectrum.

She had only looked after the Thornton baby during Eleanor's break, and hadn't taken much notice of little Cameron or his mum, except to note that he looked far too big and strong for this unit, while Mrs Thornton looked too experienced and sensible to be worrying this much.

Hmm. So maybe that meant that she was right.

As a mother of five herself, Tammy trusted the great unwritten rule of paediatrics—listen to the mothers. She'd known her third pregnancy was different two days after she had missed her period. And she'd picked up Ben's prematurity-related eye problems when his next follow-up test was weeks away.

The day around six years ago when Sarah, her eldest, then aged almost three, had innocently entertained herself by heaping three thick feather pillows on top of four-month-old Lachlan in his bassinet while Tammy had been in the bathroom, something about the quality of the silence coming from the baby's bedroom had alerted her. She'd stopped mid-moisturise, so to speak, with three blobs of white goo dotted on her face.

She'd raced down the passage and snatched the sound-muffling pillows out of the bassinet, while Sarah had started to giggle at such a funny joke—Mummy looked so silly, throwing the pillows on the floor—to find the baby red-faced and screaming healthily, thank heaven, before any damage had been done.

Yes. Very often, a mother knew.

But what did Mrs Thornton know?

She couldn't say. 'Something,' she repeated stubbornly.

Tammy began to understand why the highly intelligent, highly capable, highly non-vague and non-intuitive Dr Laird Burchell had found this particular mother so irritating and why he had opted for the doctor's privilege of passing the problem on to a lower hospital life form such as Tammy herself.

The Parry boys were behaving themselves at the moment, and she had a window of eight whole minutes before their next clustered care routine. She decided to stop for a chat beside Cameron's special premmie crib.

The rest of the unit was humming along in its usual way, the bulky pieces of medical equipment with their lines and screens and alarms dwarfing the tiny babies over whom they kept guard. There were softening touches, though. A bright toy nestled in a humidicrib or a picture taped to the transparent sides. Cards and balloons. A wall of photos of their 'graduates'—smiling toddlers who couldn't possibly have ever been so small.

'How was the pregnancy, Mrs Thornton?'

The mother nodded, understanding the intention behind the question. She was an intelligent woman. 'It was trouble-free.' She was standing, too, and rubbed her lower stomach as she spoke. She still seemed fairly sore and stiff after a powerful labour that had been abruptly ended by the emergency Caesar. 'We were in Japan for the first half of it, though, if that makes any difference.'

'Wow, Japan. That must have been interesting!' Tammy said sincerely. She'd been as far as New Zealand, on her honeymoon ten years ago, but that was about it. 'And not easy, with five kids.'

'It's a fascinating country. There was a lot to love, and a lot to adjust to, especially with the kids, as you say.'

'What were you doing there?'

'Alan—my husband—had a sabbatical. Someone organised a terrific house for us, out in the countryside. He commuted into the city. When we discovered I was pregnant again, we found a doctor who spoke English, but I found him difficult to understand. And I don't think he understood me much either.'

'Was the prenatal care similar to what we have here?'

'Mostly. As I said, it was an easy pregnancy. I only saw the doctor three times, I think, for routine checks, then we came back here when I was at about five months. I did have an ultrasound there.'

'At eighteen weeks, like we do here?'

'Yes, just under.' Mrs Thornton frowned. 'Actually, I guess it was more like fifteen weeks, if Dr Lutze was right that Cameron was at thirty-four weeks when he was born, not thirty-six weeks, like we thought. I should change his nappy,' she added.

She looked tired and uncomfortable, and Tammy found herself offering to do the change, even though she usually breathed a sigh of relief whenever a parent's help lightened the workload.

'Thanks,' Mrs Thornton said. She sat down, and confessed, 'I skipped the postnatal exercise class this morning. I'm slack!'

'You know all too well what's waiting for you at home.' Tammy grinned. 'I have five kids myself.' She was working as she spoke, deftly untaping the sides of the nappy, gently lifting the little legs and bottom.

'Then you understand!' Mrs Thornton said with feeling.

The nappy felt very light. You became pretty skilled at estimating urinary output by the weight in your hand. Dry, versus slightly wet, versus nicely soaked. This one felt dry.

'When did you last change him?' she asked his mother.

'Oh, it would be a couple of hours ago. What's the time now?'

'Almost seven-thirty.'

'That late! In that case, it's about four hours since I changed him.'

'Was he very wet then?'

'The nurse weighed the nappy. Just a few mils, she said. I think she wrote it down.' She didn't ask if the low output could be a problem, but Tammy could see she'd gone on the alert.

'Let's get you into a new one, little man,' she murmured to the baby, wondering if this could be the source of Mrs Thornton's nebulous worry. He shouldn't be dehydrated. There was no obvious distension in his lower abdomen. And newborns often didn't pee very much at first.

Still... She took his temperature, although he wasn't due for it, and found that it had gone up a few points—38.1 degrees Celsius. He was officially febrile now, and fever in a premmie newborn wasn't something you ignored.

She found Dr Burchell at the far end of the unit, studying the notes of a baby girl with a serious heart defect, and told him, 'I'm not sure if this earns me that coffee you mentioned...'

'Good coffee, right? Freshly brewed, in a china cup.'

'That's the one... Could there be a kidney problem? He doesn't seem to be putting out much urine.'

'Newborns don't.' Dr Burchell's mind was clearly still on the heart baby, whose blood gases were getting worse.

The tiny girl needed surgery, Tammy knew, but she really wasn't strong enough. They'd wanted to get her weight up higher, but it was going in the opposite direction, and her little body was exhausting itself getting that tiny, damaged heart to work.

'He's five days old,' Tammy persisted, even though she understood Dr Burchell's tight face and the frustrated way he paged through the notes and looked at the heart baby. He wanted to focus on the more serious case. 'He's started feeding. And his temp's over 38.'

OK, she had his attention now. Hopefully he wouldn't ask *how much* over 38 degrees. His grey eyes—a deep, liquid grey—fixed themselves on her cap, narrowing with something that was probably annoyance, and she wondered if bits of her hair were making an unauthorised escape bid. They often did.

'You're thinking there's a partial blockage, and he's having urinary reflux?' he asked. Grey eyes, but possibly with some chips of green in a different light, Tammy mentally revised.

'Giving him an infection, yes, that's what I'm wondering.'

He was already looking back down at the heart baby. 'Look, we'll do an ultrasound. Rule it out.'

Rule it out.

His faith in her diagnostic skills clearly wasn't high. It didn't look as if she was getting that coffee any time soon.

'Thanks, um, Tammy,' he added.

'No worries,' she told him cheerfully, and went back to her charges, prepared to think no more about it.

Eleanor had returned from her break and was gently urging Mrs Thornton to have a relaxing shower. Little Cameron's next nappy would probably weigh twice as much as a dry one, and Tammy would feel like an idiot for her rash diagnosis.

Yeah, that would be good.

She had a nagging suspicion that the kilos on her butt, the zeros in her bank account and the five kids at home might not be quite enough to keep her safe from a man like

Laird Burchell. Tall, broad-shouldered, lovely neck, not a hint of a receding hairline, intelligent and caring and capable...and then there were those deep, perceptive eyes.

He was—if you had time to take notice of such things—gorgeous. If he decided she was an idiot, therefore, so much the better.

# CHAPTER THREE

THE sprawling acreage of the Yarra Valley Garden and Landscape Centre on a Sunday morning was one of Tammy's favourite places when she'd really, seriously, drastically run out of ideas and energy at home, didn't want to spend much money, and when the playground down the road had earned a moaning chorus of, 'But we've been there three times this week.'

Mum was taking a break today, leaving her little flat behind Tammy's house temporarily empty. She deserved it about five times over, and had gone to Tammy's brother's place in Healesville for a barbecue lunch and a peaceful afternoon. His two boys were quiet lads in their late teens, and his wife—Tammy's sister-in-law Jeannette—was a terrific person and spoiled Mum rotten. She would return refreshed, and probably bearing leftovers.

The kids had a good time at the garden centre, and Tammy was able to get some time alone, even though it was only in her thoughts. But when you'd spent over an hour letting the kids chase around the big glazed pots and orchard trees and ornamental fountains, or playing name-that-flower games, or swinging your four-year-old triplets on the swings in the designated kids' area, you really owed it to the garden centre management to buy a plant.

Tammy always found it a terrible hardship to have to buy a plant.

In a more perfect world—a world where counting every penny occupied a much smaller portion of her time—she would have bought at least twelve.

That kaffir lime tree, for example. Or a pair of those cyclamens in bright lipstick colours. Some drought-tolerant grevilleas or bottlebrush. A lemon-scented eucalyptus. Oh, and herbs. She loved herbs.

She decided on a little punnet of lemon thyme, and accepted that five ice creams on sticks would have to be added to the bill. The spring sunshine had grown quite hot, and the kids were getting hungry and thirsty. The ice creams would reward them for good behaviour, and tide them over until she could get them home and make some lunch.

In the herb section, she saw a familiar figure—Laird Burchell, the last man on earth she would have expected or wanted to see here, with the possible exception of her ex-husband—and unfortunately he saw her before she could veer in the direction of the summer annuals and get out of his way.

He was wearing jeans, a blue polo shirt, a pair of scuffed work boots and a broad-brimmed Akubra hat, which made him look like a farmer. There was an air of relaxed satisfaction hovering around him that she hadn't seen on him in the NICU.

Some doctors played with their investments during their time off.

Dr Burchell apparently preferred to play at being a man of the land.

He came up to her with arrow-like directness while she stood there with garden-centre potting mix leaking out of the holes in the bottom of the lemon thyme punnet, dirtying her hands. In the background Ben knocked over a standard rose bush, and Tammy hoped she'd get a chance to set it upright again before either the garden centre staff or Laird Burchell realised that Ben was hers.

'Convenient, seeing you here,' he said.

'Oh, is it?' She smiled.

'I owe you a coffee.' He'd completely skipped hello.

She understood at once. 'You mean something did show up on Cameron Thornton's ultrasound?'

'I sent him down late last night, but you'd gone by the time he came back. There was a marked dilatation in the left kidney, suggesting a significant ureteral obstruction. He's on antibiotics, and we'll do a pyeloplasty on Monday. Mrs Thornton is not even trying to resist telling me that she told me so.'

'Well, we did take a while to trust her intuition. She's allowed to be smug.'

'But I'm hoping you'll resist telling me that *you* told me so, if I make good on the coffee deal.' He gestured behind him to the garden-centre building, where there was a pretty café section overlooking the greenery.

He meant coffee right now, Tammy realised.

Well, you could get it here in paper cups, to go.

'No paper cups, right?' he said, as if reading her thoughts and challenging them. She remembered her joking insistence that it had to be *good* coffee, in a china cup.

'That is, if you want to,' he added, just as a man who could conceivably have been her husband picked up a punnet of parsley and one of basil and moved in Tammy's direction.

'Would you rather get it over with?' she teased, letting Dr Burchell think what he liked about her relationship to the herb hunter—who wasn't her type at all.

She would have a latte, she decided, and she could sip it on one of the garden benches out the front, while the kids ate their ice creams. She'd tell Dr Burchell he didn't need to stay and keep her company. He could buy his pair of matching maidenhair ferns, or whatever, and go home to put them on his glassed-in townhouse balcony.

Meanwhile, Lachlan was trying to help Ben to set the rosebush straight. There was only a little bit of spilled soil on the ground, thank goodness. But the thorny branches of the fallen rose caught in the next rosebush as Lachlan pushed it too hard, and three of the bushes fell in a heap. They'd outgrown their pots and were top-heavy. 'Sorry, Mummy,' he mouthed, wincing.

Oh, dear! Oh, no! Now all five children were attempting to sort out the rosebushes, and Tammy could see the green overalls of a garden-centre employee approaching behind them, ready to yell.

'It's going to take more than coffee,' she said quickly to Laird. 'That's if you do mean now.'

'More than coffee?'

'Um, it's going to take five ice creams as well.'

'*Five* ice creams?'

'I mean, I'll pay for them, obviously, but you'll either have to leave at once, which I'd advise because the Prunty family is about to get into trouble, or you can sit and watch the ice creams get all over my children's— Excuse me.'

Before the fourth and fifth rosebushes could fall, she raced to the scene of rose devastation and managed to restore order, with only one resulting thorn scratch on her hand and one abject 'Sorry' to the garden-centre person, who did not look as if he had ever met a child, let alone had any of his own.

He checked meticulously and pointedly for damage, and Tammy revised her estimation of his previous experience.

He had met children before.

He ate them regularly for breakfast.

'Which ones are yours?' Laird asked, beside her. 'The kids, I mean.'

'Oh. Which ones? Of those? All of them!'

'All five?'

'Yes.' Was he turning pale? She wouldn't blame him. People often did.

'I somehow thought it was three,' he murmured.

'No, it's five.' She held up the correct number of fingers, just to drive the point home.

'You said something about three parent-teacher conferences the other day.'

'Three four-year-olds, one pre-school teacher.'

'Triplets!'

'You've turned pale.'

He really had.

*And we're looking at each other a bit more often than we should be, and holding the looks for too long. It's weird.*

'Five kids, including triplets,' she went on. 'That's why I need five ice creams. I'm not making you pay through the nose for my diagnosis of the Thornton baby by eating all five myself, I promise.'

'And you're on your own with them. In a garden centre. Five of them.' Was he horrified or impressed? She couldn't tell. 'You don't have your husband here with you, or—?'

'They're pretty good, usually. They love it here.' She added awkwardly, 'And I'm divorced,' because the husband-like herb man had wandered off and lost his usefulness as a decoy.

Although why she should have wanted Dr Burchell to think that she was still married, she wasn't sure.

Yes, she *was* sure. Extra kilos, tight budget, five kids, being an idiot, plus the presumption on his part of her possessing a current flesh-and-blood husband. In some situations, a sensible woman needed all the protection she could get.

He looked at the kids. 'Wow.'

'I know. The triplets were pregnancy number three. Naturally conceived. Bit of a shock for all concerned.'

'I bet.' He smiled, almost tentative about it. Tammy had the impression that, like the garden centre man, he hadn't met many children other than the fragile newborns he worked with and seemed to care about so much. But he definitely didn't eat kids for breakfast. 'Of course I'll get them ice cream,' he said heartily. 'I still think you're brave, bringing them here.'

'Your lips say *brave* but your face says *crazy*,' she joked. 'Sometimes, though, I go crazier staying at home.'

I'm the one who's crazy, Laird decided.

He hadn't really been obliged to resurrect the offer of coffee at all, let alone here and now, with kids and plants and ice cream. He could easily have avoided her eye, or said a brief hello in passing, or made a very plausible assumption about the matrimonial status of the man browsing through the herbs only a few feet away, and Tammy Prunty would quite acceptably have heard about Cameron Thornton's hydronephrosis on her next shift.

They would both have been off the hook.

And yet he'd pushed the issue, and let himself in for what might be a tedious or embarrassing half-hour. How long did it take children to eat ice cream? He had no idea.

He had a funny relationship with kids. Understood almost everything there was to understand about tiny premmie bodies, then waved goodbye to them as they graduated out of his care and only saw them again when proud parents brought them in weeks or months or years later to show off how they'd grown and changed. They were unrecognisable by that point, of course.

He responded to the looks on the parents' faces more than to the kids themselves, and had been wondering lately if he'd ever experience that kind of love himself.

If he wanted to.

If he'd be any good at it.

What kind of woman he'd choose as his partner in such an adventure. It *was* an adventure, he considered, as much as any more outwardly dramatic activity such as rafting down the Amazon or donning a parachute and jumping from a plane.

Somehow, Tammy gathered her brood and with three redheads and three goldy-brown ones glinting in the sun, the Prunty family made its way just ahead of Laird to the café, where he learned how insanely and irrationally difficult it could be to get five kids to make up their minds about what kind of ice cream they wanted.

The two little girls were cute, rather overshadowing their smaller triplet brother. The other boy was lively and the eldest girl very bossy, in a mother's-little-helper kind of way. At around eight years old, he guessed, she was probably starting to be genuinely useful, when she wanted to be.

Tammy chose a latte, while Laird asserted his masculinity with a double short black. 'Have something to eat, too, if you're not having ice cream,' he invited her.

He'd started to understand just how hard she must work, between her responsibilities at home and her demanding role as a nurse in the NICU, and he wanted to spoil her— which was unnecessary, because she must have plenty of other people in her life to do that. She had such a warmth and vividness about her, she couldn't be short of friends.

He expected her to say no to the suggestion of food, the way Tarsha would have done. With zero reason, Tarsha was watching her weight. And Tarsha would certainly consider that Tammy should be watching hers, but apparently she wasn't.

And thank goodness she's not, his body suddenly said.

Those smooth-skinned curves were wonderful.

'Ooh, yes!' she said enthusiastically, and chose a berry friand. Adding belatedly with a contrite, embarrassed look, 'Oh, but are you having…?'

'Yes, definitely. I'm starving.' He wasn't, but hated the idea of embarrassing her. 'Now, where do you want to sit?'

'At a table where the kids can go and drip ice cream onto the paving stones outside, and I can watch them at the same time.'

'So, this corner one, on the deck?'

'Perfect!'

He began to appreciate the presence of the kids after a few minutes.

Any time this began to feel anything like a date—which it most emphatically wasn't—Tammy would deflect the awkwardness with some instruction along the lines of, 'Lick the bottom of it, Ben, before the chocolate slides off.' She could interrupt her conversation with Laird in mid-sentence, and pick up again exactly where she'd left off, without the least apparent difficulty.

His head was soon spinning.

Her head gleamed in a shaft of sunlight.

And he had a weird, unexpectedly emphatic thought that he'd like to get her alone some time, at a proper restaurant, without the kids, so he could actually take in what she was saying, and the way she was saying it—cheerful, direct, with humour and thoughtfulness mixing like colours swirling in a kid's painting.

'Couldn't manage without Mum.'

'Do they see their dad much?' he asked.

'No. He kind of…'

'I'm sorry, I'm getting too personal.' Why? He didn't usually, with someone he didn't know well. Somehow, though, he felt as if he did know her.

'It's all right,' she said, lifting her determined chin. 'He cut himself off, that's all. Opted out. So, no, they don't see him. The triplets barely remember him. It's…yeah…not what I would have chosen for them.'

Her face darkened for a moment, and Laird sensed a lot about what she wasn't saying—the anger and betrayal she must have felt, the sense of hurt and shock and loss, the fierce protectiveness she felt for her children, who had a father who didn't care. He had to push away a violent spurt of anger towards the man, though he didn't even know his name. You didn't need to know someone personally to recognise that level of appalling behaviour.

But she added decisively, 'In some ways it's easier that he's not around.'

'Really?'

'It is.' Even firmer, convincing herself as much as him, he could tell. 'I know where I stand, not like a couple of women I know—Help him, Sarah, can you?—who can never rely on their ex-husbands taking the kids when they've said they would—No, wipe his chin, there, that's right—or bringing them back on time, or remembering where their soccer games are.' She smiled suddenly, sat up straighter, pitched her voice a little higher. 'Hey, though, did you see the new perennials they have in? Gorgeous! The bees are going crazy over the lavender in flower.'

'I'm sorry?' Did this have anything at all to do with the unreliability of ex-husbands? 'I'm not here for perennials, I'm here for a load of—'

'I was being whiny and boring,' she explained seriously—and inaccurately. 'I heard myself, and—Laura, don't drop the wrapper on the ground.'

'You weren't. Being whiny or boring.'

*And if you ever are, I can always entertain myself by looking at your hair.*

For some reason, it fascinated him. Maybe because he'd first seen her without it, when it had been hidden beneath the surgical cap, and so he hadn't realised that she was pretty.

He'd even told Tarsha that she wasn't, which now felt like a betrayal.

Tammy's hair made sense of her colouring, and of the whole shape of her face. It was like the flowers here at the garden centre. You could get away with colour combinations that would never work in clothing or paint colours. Her hair made her...he hesitated over the word, in his thoughts, but then threw caution to the winds...beautiful.

Her hair really made her beautiful.

Inconsequentially, he remembered something his mother had once said. 'Natural redheads. So unfair! They can be seventy years old, most of them, and they still won't have so much as a grey hair!'

Watching the calm, cheerful way Tammy dealt with her brood, Laird decided that she thoroughly deserved nature's reward in this area. Thirty or forty years from now, when her kids were grown and gone, she would still have the most glorious, beautiful hair.

'Decided to spare you. Let's talk about something interesting.' She looked over his shoulder. 'Ben, there's another piece going to slide off.' Ben peered at his ice cream. Tammy watched anxiously. Without taking her eyes from the little boy, she asked, 'Have you travelled much? What do you like to do when you're not saving babies? Oh, good, he's got it. What are you going to buy here today, apart from coffee and ice cream? Are you a garden nut like I am, or do you just put in a bit of decoration to maintain your property value?'

She turned back to him at last, and beamed at him, took a big bite of her friand and a sip of her latte and fixed her lively blue eyes on his face ready to listen, the way she probably listened to her kids when they talked about their day at school.

'Do I have to answer all those questions at once, or can I tackle them one at a time?'

'One at a time will do. I'll keep track of which ones you've done, tick them off, and tell you when to go on to the next.'

'You're not serious.'

'Not often. If you ask for serious, you'll be sorry, we'll really be scraping the bottom of the barrel.'

'Hmm, don't know about that. I'm open to all options at this stage.'

They smiled at each other.

Was that…a *date*?

Surely not.

Leaving the garden centre, Tammy was flustered and sort of mushy inside for reasons completely unrelated to Laird Burchell—delirious excitement about going home to plant the lemon thyme, perhaps. Nothing to do with that lovely half-hour—longer, actually—that she'd just spent having coffee with the man.

Coffee that hadn't been a date.

'I mean, it just *wasn't*,' she muttered to herself, shovelling the kids into the van. 'Or if it was, it must have been the date from hell, as far as he was concerned.'

Even though he hadn't let it show.

He'd been…well, gorgeous, actually.

Yes, that word again.

Smiling at her. Relaxing sideways in the wrought-iron café chair with his legs crossed at his ankles, those big work boots clunky and heavy on his feet, and his elbow on the table, as if he wasn't a rapidly rising neonatal specialist at one of the state's best hospitals. Picking up a paper napkin one of the girls had dropped, even though it had been all sticky and sodden with ice cream and had immediately stuck in shreds to his fingers. Ploughing gamely on with what he'd been saying, even when the kids had needed her attention in the middle of a sentence, three sentences in a row.

Then, when it had been time to leave, instead of the token piece of greenery she'd expected him to take home, he'd pointed to a large truck filled with orchard trees and young eucalypts and acacias. 'That's my lot heading off now. I'd better get ahead of it, so I can direct the driver where to go.'

'*All* of it? The whole truckful?'

'I have a piece of land just up the valley.'

'A hobby farm?' she guessed.

'Well, a bit bigger than that.' He gave her a stern, re-proachful look.

Him? A hobby farm? Please! As if that fitted with the dignity of a good-looking and well-built medical specialist.

'More of an investment,' he stressed. 'A vineyard. It should start turning a profit within the next couple of years. Meanwhile, there are a couple of acres around the house that need more trees.' Then he confessed with a wry grin, 'You're completely right, though, I should be more honest with myself. I own the place for fun more than money—such a change to get dirty instead of keeping watch on the scrupu-lous sterility in the NICU—which makes it a hobby farm.'

'I didn't mean that to sound rude.'

'It didn't. It just sounded upfront. I'm going to embrace the truth from now on, with my eyes open. I, Dr Laird Burchell, have a hobby farm.'

'What did you say, Mummy?' Sarah asked.

'Nothing, love.' Oh, dear, had Sarah heard that muttering a few seconds ago about the date from hell?

'Who was that man?'

'Just one of the doctors. I gave him a good suggestion about one of the babies at the hospital, so he bought us the coffee and ice cream to say thank you.'

'Did he pay?'

'Yes, he did.' Even though she'd tried to protest about his offer, probably for too long.

'So we saved money.'

'Yes, sweetheart, we did.'

Nearly twenty dollars.

Tammy didn't even try to pretend to herself that she wasn't counting. Twenty dollars would pay for a school excursion each for Sarah and Lachlan, or several DVD rentals, or the part of a GP's bill that the government didn't cover.

It was a challenge, living on such a tight budget, but Tammy refused to let it get her down. She liked challenges. She liked the small, regular victories over her finances that came from things like making pizza at home instead of succumbing to the enticing odours of the local Italian place, or putting hot-water bottles in the kids' beds on a cold winter night instead of running the expensive electric wall heaters.

It was all about attitude.

Which brought her back to Laird Burchell, their coffee and their much-interrupted conversation.

Definitely and absolutely not a date.

Not the right attitude for such a thing, in either of them. *But I liked it.*

'He's so-o-o nice,' Sarah said.

'Is he?' she asked absently.

'Because he paid.'

Sarah was such a canny thing, Tammy thought with a pang. Even though she tried not to speak ill of Tom in the kids' hearing, her eldest daughter somehow knew how much her dad had let them all down—how much he was still letting them down by never seeing them and sending those erratic, unpredictable child-support payments.

He knew her well enough to guess just when his unreliability would have pushed her to the edge of her tolerance, so that she'd start seriously thinking of taking him to court, and then a cheque would come. It hurt a lot to think that he'd use his understanding of her that way.

She'd talked about this to a couple of friends recently— Mel and Bron—and as usual they'd taken her side too heartily, indignant at what a rat he was. She hugely appreciated the way they stuck up for her...and she wished they wouldn't. Mostly, she tried not to talk to her friends about Tom. It was safer, somehow, to keep her darker feelings and her vulnerabilities to herself.

And, Tammy discovered, she wasn't thinking about Tom as she drove home. She was thinking about the sun on the garden-centre plants, and Laird Burchell's vivid descriptions of Egypt and Japan, his cheerful admission to indulging in a hobby farm for the pleasure of getting dirty and the way he hadn't seemed nearly as appalled by her rabble of children as she would have expected.

*I'm in trouble...*

Another realisation that she immediately knew she wasn't going to share with friends who cared about her too much.

Or Mum.

To take out yet more insurance against being completely ridiculous, Tammy ate an extra piece of cake on top of her sandwich lunch. Five kids, and two more kilos on her butt, to counteract the fact that she'd been right about the Thornton baby and therefore Laird Burchell wouldn't be able to conclude she was an idiot.

But she was worrying about it for nothing. The cake was unnecessary. No man in his right mind would be remotely interested in her.

Laird drove out to the vineyard in a daze and arrived ahead of the truck containing his trees. Knowing they'd be here any minute, he waited out front, ready to point in the direction of the arrangement of pre-dug holes. Hell, where was the plan he'd sketched out? Which tree went into which hole? He'd thought he had it clear in his head but for the moment it seemed to have gone.

To be replaced by bright, dizzying visions of Tammy Prunty.

He kept thinking about the way the sun had shone on her hair. She must have washed it that morning, because every time she'd moved her head, it had bounced or swung or slid over her ear, rippling and shimmering like a shampoo commercial. He could see it in his memory, and it gave him a bright flash of pleasure every time. Her smile and her eyes, the way she looked at her children, the moments of self-doubt he'd read in the set of her shoulders and the tilt of her head.

The whole morning seemed drenched in colour. The sky, the vivid greenery, the glossy chocolate of the kids' ice creams melting in the sun. The vivid oranges and yellows and greens of the fruits forming on the new citrus trees, which were currently wending their way in the truck up his long drive.

Into his mind there flashed another image—Tammy opening her mouth to bite into Lachlan's ice cream.

'Want a taste, Mummy?' he'd generously asked.

She'd answered, 'Thank you, sweetheart,' given him a hug and taken a small chunk of lurid turquoise bubblegum-flavour ice cream between her surprisingly dainty white teeth. 'Mmm, yummy!'

She'd leaned forward so as not to risk the ice cream dripping onto her summery cream vest top, and for a moment he'd glimpsed the lavishly full slopes of her breasts, as creamy white and smooth as the rest of her skin and edged with a couple of token pieces of lace. He'd looked quickly down at his coffee, but somehow the memory had imprinted itself in his mind and he couldn't seem to let it go.

*I want her. In my bed. In my life.*

In his damned garden!

It wasn't possible. Here he was, waiting for his trees as the truck slowed to negotiate a final bend, thinking lustful, rosy-edged thoughts about a curvy divorced mother of five who'd narrowly escaped spilling ice cream down her chin.

And yet he felt as if someone had hit him over the back of the head with a brick and he was seeing stars...along with her blue eyes, red hair and sumptuous figure.

He couldn't remember ever feeling this way before in his life. Knocked sideways. Without warning.

He must have had the experience before. Surely. Or else

the feeling itself had something fatally wrong with it. Someone had drugged his coffee, or he was getting sick, or he'd temporarily taken leave of his senses.

He couldn't be falling in love with her. Not so fast. Not on so little foundation. Not with someone so flagrantly impossible and unlikely. Had that it's-not-you-it's-me conversation with Tarsha the other night come as more of a disappointment than he'd honestly acknowledged to himself? Was he just an unattached male approaching middle age and getting desperate? Neither possibility rang true, despite some strenuous theorising.

The truck ground to a halt in front of him, and the driver wound down his window to speak, wanting to know where to go next. Laird directed him around the side of the house and the plan for the trees re-formed itself in his head, which made him feel a lot better. With the driver, his sidekick and Laird himself all working hard, they put the trees into the correct holes in ten minutes, and Laird himself spent the rest of the day shovelling in dirt and composted manure and mulch until the job was done.

There was something about tree roots and fresh soil and hard work. The sudden, raging fever called *falling in love with Tammy* settled down considerably during the course of the afternoon and he ended the day confident that he had it under control. He didn't want it and didn't trust it and it didn't make sense, therefore it wasn't real or significant, and would soon fade.

But that night, he dreamed about her—a triple X-rated dream that ended much too soon and left him lying awake afterwards for an hour.

He didn't know what was happening to him.

* * *

'It's supposed to be a brilliant collection,' Tarsha said, the following Thursday night.

She'd asked him if he would accompany her to the opening of an exhibition—'be my handbag,' as she'd phrased it—and he'd agreed, as promised.

'Look good, won't you?' she'd cajoled him on the phone. 'People will be there. I need to impress.'

So here they were, impressing like crazy, in a crush of other people doing the same thing as they wandered around the museum-quality collection of costumes from the star-studded history of the Australian film industry.

Laird took an hors d'oeuvre and examined his own profound state of dissatisfaction with a critical eye. He was bored. He felt instinctively hostile to almost every woman he saw…and even more hostile to the ones he actually talked to…because they were all too rich or too thin or too self-obsessed or—

Because they weren't Tammy Prunty, basically, and because he couldn't kid himself for a second that they were anything like her. This was what it boiled down to, and he was horrified about the strength of his feelings on the subject. For heaven's sake, he barely knew the woman.

*You know enough*, said a part of him he hadn't known existed, and that he didn't trust.

'Earth to Laird,' Tarsha drawled. The crush had begun to thin. The hors d'oeuvre platters and wineglasses were emptying. People had started to leave. 'Where are you tonight? You're miles away.'

'Sorry.'

'Work?'

'No. Not work. Well, sort of.'

one at work?' she shrewdly guessed.

es. Someone at work.' Someone who filled out a
scrub suit very, very well, and who hid what was
her best feature under her cap. 'It's OK. Go and
meone important.'

you're being nice enough to pull handbag duty,
ress an interest in your life. Besides,' she added
less honesty, 'the important people are leaving
I've talked to them already. Tell me about this
t work.'

er said it was a—'

gave a knowing smile. 'I read the look on your
didn't have to.'

ale perception was his undoing.

tic, Tarsha. I think I could be falling in love with
tal words fell from his lips as if spoken in the
l.

ded crazy, even to his own ears, and he com-
stood Tarsha's sceptical tilt of the head. 'Then
her for a while…' she murmured thoughtfully.
ry long at all.'

him, he told her everything…

nse and well-articulated cautions carried
he exhibition opening in a better frame
as sure, for a whole eleven hours, that
m licked.

ee you getting into some awful situation,

'You said yourself you hardly know her.'

True again.

'That kind of mismatched relationship is unf
people involved, and with all those kids…'

Once again, hard to argue.

He arrived in the NICU at six-forty on Frida
after a good night's sleep, ready to focus on the
babies, convinced it was going to be a good day
Tarsha's warnings about the temporary insani
knocked-sideways feeling about Tammy Prun
phorically clutched to his chest like a protective

The suggestion she could be a gold-digger he'
to, but Tarsha had told him, 'Gold-diggers do
come with bleached hair and fake boobs.'

'Mmm, she doesn't need those…'

'OK, so she's not a gold-digger.'

'No, but I take your point.'

'You do have family money, and that ver
ment property.'

'Well, hobby farm.'

'But even if she's not a gold-digger, I c
half a dozen scenarios here, and they all e

Laird definitely didn't want anything th
There were enough of those in the NIC
bright photos of healthy babies on their
seem bright enough. They'd had a ne
night. Normal full-term pregnancy, m
twenties, and then a baby born with a stru
a list of abnormalities that suggested a rare

The parents wanted answers and reassuranc

could give those yet. For the moment they were treating the symptoms, going through the literature and deciding on tests.

On his way to take his first look at the baby, Laird passed Tammy with another new mother—a teenager, out of her depth, who'd given birth to a baby with intrauterine growth retardation. The little boy had needed breathing support but he was doing well enough now to be out of his cot and in his mother's arms.

Tammy was asking the mother about breast-feeding. He heard a whole two lines of their conversation, but that was enough.

'I'm not sure if I could handle it,' said the teenage mum.

'You never know about something until you try it,' said Tammy gently, her head bent towards the tiny swaddled bundle in the young mother's arms, her voice full of its usual warmth and hope and spirit and music.

Tarsha's arguments fragmented in Laird's head like tissue paper in water, leaving only Tammy. His memories of the morning at the garden centre. His growing reliance on her efficiency and dedication at work. The way she looked, and the way she sounded. The way she tasted her son's bubble-gum ice cream and managed to act as if she liked it.

*You never know about something until you try it.*

Against all logic, that was exactly what he was going to do. Try it. Follow this dizzying new feeling to see where it led. Because Tammy was right. More right than Tarsha. You never knew until you tried.

# CHAPTER FOUR

'WE'LL have to increase his ventilator settings,' Laird said.

'He's teetering on the edge, isn't he?' Tammy murmured. 'Are we calling it renal failure?'

Every baby in the unit had seemed to go through a medical crisis in the last week, and so far the next week didn't look as if it would be much better.

Adam Parry's kidneys hadn't yet begun to work properly, and if they didn't do so soon, he wouldn't survive. The Thornton baby had had his pyeloplasty to correct the blocked ureter. He was recovering, but his little system didn't like the antibiotics so he wasn't eating well.

Worst of all, little Riley, the sickest of the Vitelli triplets, had died, his bowel destroyed by necrotising enterocolitis and his brain suffering a second major bleed, despite Laird trying every treatment strategy in the book.

With the dark roots growing out of her untended blonde hair, Alison Vitelli had dragged herself back from Riley's heart-breaking funeral to be with her surviving two babies, and Tammy just couldn't look at the anguished expression on her face without getting a lump in her throat.

Now, Sunday evening, Adam Parry had reached the ten-day milestone, but he was swollen with fluid. His kidneys had begun to pass tiny amounts of urine—three millilitres on Friday, five yesterday, but none overnight, another few millilitres today. It wasn't enough.

His stressed and worn-out parents had gone to snatch a rare meal away from the hospital. Tammy had left her mother at home, putting the kids to bed, and had driven the new, blessedly shorter commute to work, gearing herself up for a twelve-hour overnight shift.

She'd found Laird in the unit, moving back and forth between several very ill babies and frowning in a way that made her want to reach her fingertips up and smooth out his brow.

'We're not calling it renal failure to the parents,' he answered her. 'But if his kidney function doesn't improve soon, there's not much hope. I want to see ten mils a day, minimum.'

There was almost nothing they could do. Baby Adam had been started on small amounts of breast milk—a millilitre every four hours, less than you'd feed a newborn orphaned kitten.

At least Max was doing better.

Although the most at risk immediately after birth, he'd strengthened fast. His heart was still enlarged, but the open duct had closed on its own and he'd been taken off the ventilator and put on CPAP—continuous positive airway pressure. Like his brother, he was being fed breast milk in tiny amounts, two millilitres every two hours, and soon he should be able to move into the high dependency unit. Fingers crossed, it wouldn't be that much longer until he went home.

Laird stayed watching Adam while Tammy wrote some

figures down on his chart. She sensed that Laird had something to say. There was something about the movements of his hands and the uneven sound of his breathing. An in-breath, as if he was preparing to speak, and then a controlled sigh.

Something was on his mind. She steeled herself to hear it—some heroic, experimental intervention he would suggest for Adam, which she couldn't believe would do any good. The little boy was too frail. They just had to count those precious millilitres, hold their breath and wait.

Tammy was literally holding hers, waiting for what Laird would say.

And she could feel his presence like a…a time bomb, or something.

Ticking.

Dangerous.

Ready to blow something apart.

She'd been thinking about him too much since that morning at the garden centre a week ago. Wondering what he was doing at certain moments of the day, wondering if he'd planted all those orchard trees and eucalypts himself or if he'd had fleets of burly gardeners to help, remembering the way he'd smiled, hearing his voice and thinking of questions she wanted to ask him.

Tammy herself was the thing getting blown apart, as it turned out.

'I've been wondering if you'd like a repeat of that coffee,' he said finally, almost knocking her off her feet with the unexpectedness of it, shattering her composure, sending her emotions flying. 'We didn't get much of a chance to talk last weekend. Or, at least, when we did it was mostly to the kids.'

He gave a slow grin. 'Felt as if I'd got off lightly. You should at least have had a refill on your latte.'

'You don't have to do this, Dr Burchell.'

*Why* are you doing it? We've already had our date-that-wasn't-a-date. You saved me twenty dollars.

What was it that musketeer types said in times gone by, after a duel? *Honour is satisfied.* Well, it had been, in this case, on both sides.

'Please stop calling me that, Nurse Prunty,' he said, in a tone of studied, teasing patience.

It rattled her. He *wasn't* flirting. And if he was, she didn't want him to…and yet she liked it. Really, really liked it. Hated herself for liking it, but felt helpless to do a thing about her reaction.

'I mean, I wasn't serious to begin with, about the coffee deal,' she blurted out, feeling her face begin to burn. 'The Thornton baby's hypernephrosis was a lucky guess, that's all. And you've made good on it anyhow. One latte. Five ice creams. Honour is satisfied.'

He laughed at that last bit and she wished she hadn't said it. Maybe it wasn't what duelists said at all. Was he laughing *with* her or *at* her? What should she trust? Her gut or her head?

She saw his eyes fix on her face, and looked down at Adam Parry's chart to escape their cool, intent, grey light. It didn't work. She could feel that he was still looking at her, and that he was seeing too much. Too much of the heat. Too much of the mixed emotions. Too much of the giddy awareness. Too much of her soul.

What else did he want to say? Hadn't she let him off the hook, if not all that gracefully?

Take the out I'm offering, Dr Burchell, please!

Tom's desertion, not just from their marriage but from any supporting role in her life, had rocked her so much. She didn't want this kind of a challenge, didn't want her hard-won equilibrium rocked in such an unexpected way. Didn't want to have to be brave enough to trust a man again.

Not now.

And maybe never. Wasn't she brave enough in so many other ways? Settling into the role of aging family matriarch had real appeal.

Nonsense, said her hormones, her nerve-endings, her heart. You're young. You're a woman. You *want*.

Love and adventure and newness and safety and, yes, sex.

'OK,' he said finally, and she began to breathe again as he walked away.

While, all right, at the same time fighting this stupid, stupid disappointment because she hadn't permitted herself to jump at the offer, whether he'd meant it or not.

Great, Tammy, accept a duty offer of coffee with a man who's so far out of your league he's not even playing the same football code. Remember those kilos on your butt! They're there for a reason!

They managed to get away from each other's awkward auras at last. She busied herself with the Parry twins and he busied himself with other babies, and at some point he must have left because she looked up, cautiously, then looked around searchingly, and couldn't see him anywhere.

*Thank goodness.*

*I wish he'd come back.*

Oh, Tammy, you fool!

For the next five days, while tiny Adam's kidney

function slowly and precariously improved, she was aware of Laird whenever they met up in the unit and she hated it. Why did she always look for him? Why did she keep a running note of where he was, when he arrived, when he left? Why had her ears tuned themselves so precisely to the sound of his voice? Why did she remember every word they said to each other and replay whole conversations over to herself in bed at night and driving home?

And she hated it all the more because surely he could see her reaction.

Her skin always showcased the slightest blush, especially when she was wearing a cap to confine her hair. The movements they all made around these babies were so quiet and careful, the slightest piece of clumsiness in his presence—*because* of his presence—was magnified to elephant size. It was never anything more than a fluttering of her fingers at the wrong moment, or a hesitation over a monitor setting, but around these babies, those things showed.

She was terrible at hiding her feelings, especially the unwanted, negative ones.

The only answer was to go on the attack with her best weapon—humour.

Yet somehow even this deserted her, and everything she said in his hearing was lame and silly to her ears.

By the time she finished her fourth shift for the week, at three o'clock on Friday afternoon, every nerve had frayed at the edges.

Adam Parry had been taken off those heartbreakingly small doses of breast milk, because his bowel wasn't coping, so the mood was tense as afternoon nurses handed over to evening staff. Fran sat slumped beside him, only moving when she went to spend some time with Max. She'd lost her pregnancy weight and more since the birth.

'Is it confirmed that he has NEC?' Tammy's replacement asked, well away from the mother's hearing.

'Not yet. We're still hoping. Just giving his bowel a rest and hoping it'll start working soon. His kidneys are still a real worry, too.'

'Shoot!' said the other nurse. 'And they're such good parents! They're both wearing themselves out.'

'When are you on again, Tammy?' asked another nurse, Dorinda, as they left the unit together and headed for the lift.

'Monday.'

'Same here. And I'm going away with my husband for the weekend.' Dorinda made a jazzy movement with her hips.

'I've got a whole two hours, which sounds as good as a weekend to me, right now. Sarah and Lachlan are going to friends after school, and the triplets have a party until five.'

'Going to do something good? Buy shoes?'

'Yeah, right. Buy some killer heels, have a Fijian sugar massage, browse through expensive antique malls and load up on extravagant amounts of jewellery.'

The other nurse stopped in her tracks suddenly, and swore.

Tammy gave her an inquisitive look and stopped, too, just as Laird caught up to them metres from the lift. For once, her ultra-sensitive Laird Burchell radar had switched itself off, and she hadn't realised he was behind them. She blushed instantly now that she knew he was there, of course.

He pressed the lift button, while Dorinda explained,

'Letter to post. Left it on the desk in the unit.' She was already heading back for it. 'Thanks for mentioning antiques, or I wouldn't have remembered.'

'The letter is about antiques?'

Dorinda was already halfway down the corridor. 'No, tenants at my mother's damaged the furniture, letter to the real-estate people,' she called back. 'Doesn't make sense, but it just connected in my head somehow. Antiques, furniture, letter. You know how it is.'

Tammy was left alone with Laird, waiting for the lift.

In silence.

Getting hot all over.

Cursing herself for being such a fool.

'Instead of antique malls or a massage, how about that coffee today?' he said, just before the lift arrived.

'I was just joking about all that. I wasn't really going to have a massage.'

'I didn't think you were,' he replied, his tone deceptively mild. 'Probably counts as time and money spent on yourself, and you're not allowed any of that.'

She looked at him, open-mouthed. How did he know?

'Not my business?' he said.

His smile was *sneaky*. Yes! Downright sneaky! No man had a right to smile like that, so wide and white and twinkly and gorgeous, when she was trying so hard to stay immune. It wasn't fair.

'Nope,' she replied, not letting her voice go breathy. 'It's not your business.'

'Is that why you said no to coffee the other day?' he persisted. 'Because it was something for you, not something for the kids?' The interrogation was lazy, the way a cat could almost lazily play with a mouse. 'That's the theory I've been working on.'

She made a helpless sound. 'No. Yes. Probably. Partly.'

'And what's the reason you're saying no today? I'm right, aren't I? You're saying no?'

'Yes.'

'Oh, you're saying yes?'

He knew she wasn't!

'No. I'm saying no.' Gritted teeth. Melting stomach.

'So…?'

'Because I have to go home and make casseroles to freeze.'

'So you'll make one less casserole. Reason not accepted.'

'Because you don't have to do this,' she burst out. 'You really don't! The Thornton baby was a lucky guess, and he's doing really well in the SCBU now, which is great, so it's over. We've been through this conversation.'

'I know I don't have to do it. That's not why I'm asking. Which we've also been through. Do you really think I'd ask you for coffee out of duty and obligation?'

'OK, then I'm saying no because I don't *know* why you're asking!' When desperate, try honesty. Puts 'em off every time. 'I can't think why any man would possibly want to invite me, Tammy Prunty, NICU nurse and divorced mother of five, out for coffee. Let alone a man like you!' she finished, in danger of starting to yell.

She hadn't counted on him using the same weapon on her.

The honesty thing.

He leaned against the wall and sighed, rubbed a sore spot on the back of his neck with his long, capable fingers. 'Yeah, I don't quite understand it either.'

The lift came, with a couple of people already inside.

He shook his head and frowned when they stepped back to let him and Tammy inside, and the lift doors closed again. The light on the lift button went off and neither of them pressed it to summon another one. The corridor was empty.

'On paper, you're right,' he said. 'There's a definite difference in professional status between us, as well as in life circumstances. I've never been married, I have no kids. You're probably struggling to make ends meet, while I don't know anything about how that feels. We must be roughly the same age.' He shrugged. 'Which means nothing. So I'm at a loss.'

'See?' She wrapped her arms protectively across the front of her body, aware of every movement he made, every shifting expression in his eyes, every line of his body, lolling so thoughtfully and dangerously against that wall beside the lift. Her skin was tingling, her breathing had gone shallow.

'It's got a fair bit to do with your hair, I know that,' Laird continued, sounding thoughtful. 'The fact that I didn't even know what colour it was the first time we worked together. It made me curious. And then when I did see it, it was so fabulous and rich and alive. It made you beautiful.'

'Oh...'

*Beautiful?*

Her breath caught.

'But, of course, the fact that I find you beautiful can't be the only thing. Help me out here.' She watched his mouth, the way it moved with each word. 'What is it about you, Tammy Prunty, that makes me want to find out more?' He was grinning now, inviting her to share the joke, but she couldn't.

Had he really just called her beautiful? Was there a problem with his eyes?

'I have not the slightest clue!' Her voice shook.

'So let's just do it, have the coffee, and maybe after it I'll be able to tell you. A whole list of factors. In bullet points. Triaged according to their severity.'

'No. No. Please.' She flapped her hands and refused to respond to his humour. 'I have to make the casseroles, or I'm condemning Mum to cooking half of next week. I—I don't want you sitting there trying to decide why you like me. Or if you like me. Because you probably don't. Not the way you're suggesting. Seem to be suggesting. I'm a good nurse. I'm an overworked single parent. I'm *not* beautiful.'

'Tammy—'

'Occasionally, I make use of both those sides of me— mother and nurse—and it helps me work out what's going on with the bubs and the mums. Like last week. Mrs Thornton. Which led to...' she waved her hands again, in a big, loopy spiral '...this. But there honestly isn't a lot more to me than that, so let's just leave it.'

*Before there's any risk I'll get hurt...*

She reached out and pressed the lift button, and it pinged half a second later to announce the opening of the doors, as if the hospital's unpredictable and overworked lift system was suddenly on her side.

Except, of course, Laird was going down, too, so he stepped in right behind her.

But it did break the mood, and there were already three people on board.

He didn't push her any further.

Not for another four days.

This time, he happened to find her alone in the break room. She gasped and backed against the fridge when she saw him, and the whole movement must have looked quite nutty. Paranoid. They worked together. They saw each other all the time.

He said, 'OK, make it tea, then.'

'Tea?'

'Since coffee's such a terrible idea.'

And suddenly they were laughing at each other, with a powerful edge of something much more sensual behind the laughter, before she'd even taken another breath.

'The original agreement was coffee.' Pretending to be angry. How about that? Would that work? 'And I'm really starting to worry about the health of your memory, Laird, because we've already had it at the garden centre.'

'Listen, will you stop pretending you think this is still about the Thornton baby?' he said softly. 'You know it isn't. He's gone home.'

'I'll stop pretending when you stop asking me out for coffee. For any kind of hot or cold caffeinated beverage in a restaurant-style setting,' she added quickly, sensing he was about to become pedantic.

'OK, dinner, then.'

Just as she'd thought. Pedantic. Which two could play at. 'When you stop asking me out *anywhere*.'

There was a beat of stubborn silence, then he said simply, 'I would, if I thought you really didn't want to.'

'And what makes you think I do?'

'You know.'

'I—I don't.'

'Really want me to spell it out?' This time he didn't wait

for an answer, just ticked off the list on his fingers. 'Your cheeks get pink when you see me. Your voice is pitched higher.' He looked at her mouth, and the look was like a caress. 'Your breathing makes your chest go up and down in little jerks. You start making bad jokes. Which I even find funny, because this is my problem, too. I think my chest goes up and down and my cheeks get pink.'

'No, not that, but your eyes…' She stopped. What ridiculous thing could she possibly say about his lovely grey eyes?

'You *want* to have coffee with me, Tamara Elizabeth Prunty, née Leigh,' he argued softly. 'Yes, I looked you up on the hospital database. Coffee, dinner, whatever. Only there's something telling you that you're not allowed to, apparently, and I want to find out what it is, because it is really starting to bug me!'

'You looked me up?'

'I know. I questioned it, too.'

'What answer did you get?'

'That a dinner invitation was required. It's *required*, Tammy.' His voice dropped again, to that cajoling, just-the-two-of-us pitch that shocked her to the bone every time…

*He's talking like that for me? For someone like me?*

And that she couldn't resist. 'One way or another, it's necessary,' he continued. 'Even if that's all it is. One dinner. One disappointing dinner, I guess it would have to be, or we'd want a second one. But let's not get ahead of ourselves there. Let's just…get it over with.'

Oh, she had to laugh at that!

'Get it over with? All right, and I'll grit my teeth and hold my nose, Laird, the whole way through the meal.'

# CHAPTER FIVE

LAIRD had arranged to pick Tammy up at her house at seven on Friday night, and here he was, driving down her street at two minutes to seven, looking for her house and wondering if the spell would be broken the moment he entered it.

Now, wouldn't that be convenient?

*Yeah, but I don't want it to happen.*

There was some kind of crisis going on in the Prunty household, he discovered before he'd even rung the doorbell. He heard Tammy's voice, urgently raised, and a child in tears, and frantic, thumping footsteps. Imagining an accident, he put his finger on the bell and let it peal, primed to come riding heroically to the rescue.

And was then left in no doubt as to the desirability of his arrival at that particular moment when he heard Tammy wailing, 'Oh, no, is it seven already? That can't be him! Maybe it's someone else...'

Images of himself performing some masterful medical intervention on a temporarily damaged child faded. One of the triplets—Laura?—answered the door and told him in a serious little voice, 'Mummy flooded the laundry.'

'No, Sarah, I said towels,' he heard Tammy say. 'Not teatowels, big ones. Beach towels. You know the drill with this, sweetheart, don't you? Oh, it's gone all across the floor! Has someone answered the door?'

'It's the ice-cream man,' Laura—or Lucy?—yelled to her mother. Laird followed the four-year-old until he reached the edge of the flood waters and found his lady companion for the evening.

'The *ice-cream* man?' Tammy whirled around. 'Oh, it is you! It's not quite seven yet, is it? Oh, lord, yes, it is. Hi! Um, hi.' She smiled, and tried to use her elbow to wipe something imaginary from her flushed cheek because both her hands were full.

She was still in the blue surgical scrubs she'd worn to work today, and they had wet patches all down the front. Clashing gloriously with her pink cheeks, her hair was in a copper frenzy, and bits of it were wet, too. Occupying both hands was a heavy, sodden towel, which she held over a bucket, twisting and squeezing.

'I'm not ready,' she added.

'No, really?' he drawled.

'I'm sorry. That was…more than obvious, wasn't it? This happens. I have an eight-kilogram top-loading washing-machine. Really good for a big family. It holds a heck of a lot of water, on the maximum load setting. There's one of those black plastic pipes that drains it into the laundry sink. But sometimes the pipe gets knocked out of the sink and hangs down in the gap between the machine and the sink, or the sink gets blocked by a rag and overflows. I'm feeling a need to explain on this ludicrous level of detail, by the way, because I just know nothing like this has ever happened to you in your whole entire life.'

'Well, the holes with my new trees planted in them were drowned by the rain last week, so half of them developed an unacceptable degree of lean.'

'Not the same.'

'No, not really.'

'You probably didn't even know there were eight-kilogram top-loading washing-machines.'

'My life has been the poorer for it.'

'And somehow I'm *always* upstairs or in the garden when it happens, and water gushes all over the floor before one of the kids hears the splashing noise and tells me the laundry's flooded again.'

'Seems to me that it's more than just the laundry.' The shiny expanse of water looked vast.

'The floor isn't very level.' She gestured to the shallow river that headed across the family room, into the kitchen, under the jutting, family-sized fridge, out the other side and onto the living-room carpet that started beyond the open kitchen door.

Sarah arrived with her arms full of towels.

'Just spread them over the puddle, love, so we can stop the water getting to the carpet.'

'I think it's too late for that,' Laird said, bending down to help.

'Don't,' Tammy ordered. 'You're so nicely dressed. While I'm...' She looked down at herself, then finished succinctly, 'Not.'

'Let me clean this up while you get ready.'

'No, no.' She dropped the sodden towel in the bucket

and began helping Sarah with the fresh ones. Her dryer would be chugging all night. Laird caught a glimpse of the cramped laundry room behind her and discovered she didn't have a dryer. Correction, then. Her back-yard clothesline would be draped with towels like a circus tent tomorrow. 'I know the system, you see,' she said.

'There's a system?'

'If you dam the water in the wrong place, it spreads under the stove as well, and then I can't get to it properly to mop it up. The floorboards'll rot if this keeps happening.'

'Right. So I should...?'

'Find out why Ben's crying.'

Which he'd been doing since Laird's arrival, he realised. Not letting on that he found it slightly daunting to contemplate probing the inner emotional life of a four-year-old boy, he searched for the source of the sobbing, and found Ben in the living-room, with a dogeared TV guide in front of him and a world-weary six-year-old brother ignoring his woe.

The six-year-old was Lachlan, Laird remembered. He greeted the boys and made sure they remembered who he was. The ice cream man, right? From the garden centre? Three weekends ago? Then he got down to kid level and asked Lachlan quietly, 'Do we know why he's crying?'

It wasn't from physical pain, he recognised that much.

'His show isn't on tonight.'

'His show?'

'On TV, the pet show. It says in the TV guide that it's on, but it's not, they've got something else. He says I've got the wrong channel, but I haven't and now he's upset.'

'He really likes that pet show!' He turned to Ben, who still seemed inconsolable.

What did you say at a time like this?

*Cheer up, maybe it'll be on tomorrow night instead.*

Inadequate.

*Want some ice cream?*

No, he was multi-faceted. He couldn't be just the ice cream man. When you embarked on the Amazonian rafting adventure of getting to know someone else's kids, you needed more than one way to steer the boat. And, anyway, Tammy might not believe in distractions and bribes of that nature. He didn't yet know enough about her parenting strategies.

Did he want to find out? Did he *really*? The sense of dauntingness—OK, it wasn't a real word—overtook him suddenly, and he remembered everything that Tarsha had said, all those sensible warnings about mismatched couples and things ending in tears. He didn't want to make Tammy cry.

Take her for dinner and then step away, he decided. Get your feet back on the ground. Don't hurt her. Think of all the reasons why this can't possibly work.

And, for now, tackle Ben.

'Hi, Ben,' he said.

Ben looked up. 'The guide says it's on, but it's not.'

'Shall I check the guide, just to make sure?' Laird reached out for it. 'Maybe Lachlan read the time wrong.'

'I already checked.'

'Can you read, Ben?'

The little boy nodded, while Lachlan said generously, 'He's not as bad as you'd think, for a four-year-old.'

Laird was impressed. He checked the guide anyway, but the boys were right. The pet show should have been on, but it wasn't. 'Did Mummy teach you to read?' he asked.

Ben had almost stopped crying, but not quite. Lachlan answered for him. 'He just learnt. Mummy did the letters with the triplets, and Ben started putting them together to read words.'

'That's really good, Ben. You like animals, hey?'

He nodded.

There was a knock at the back door. Laird wondered if he should answer it, but it opened at once and he heard a voice uncannily like Tammy's saying, 'Yoo-hoo, Grandma's here!'

Tammy herself appeared, even wetter down the front but a little calmer. She saw that Ben had stopped crying, and mouthed, 'Thanks,' although Laird felt he hadn't done much. Aloud, she said, 'I'll go and get ready. I'm sorry about this. Leave everything to Mum now, won't you?'

Laird introduced himself to her mother, who was clearly a lovely woman—a natural redhead, around sixty years old—which made it perfectly understandable and reasonable that she would proceed to cast him dagger-like glances of suspicion every thirty seconds.

What was he doing, going out with her divorced daughter? Would she have to beat him severely around the head and shoulders with her handbag, or something more violent? If Tammy's mum had her way, any tears involved in this whole situation would be his own, Laird realised.

And she was right to feel that way. Whatever happens, he vowed, I can't hurt her. I won't. Whatever it takes, I refuse to hurt her.

Tammy arrived back downstairs ten minutes later.

And, of course, she didn't look anything like the way Tarsha would have looked.

*Because she looks better*, said a rebellious new voice inside Laird's head. Not the way he was supposed to be thinking at all. He attempted to firm his resolve.

How would Tarsha herself have tallied up Tammy's appearance?

Ten points for the attractively piled-up hair, minus five for the strands that were already escaping down to her bare neck. Laird liked the strands, though. They whispered against her fine skin the way a man's lips would do.

Zero points for the shoes, because they were black while her dress was midnight blue, but Laird would personally have scored the shoes quite highly because Tammy could actually walk in them, swift and skimming and graceful, without either wincing or risking permanent damage to her feet.

Make-up? Minimal, but then he would have argued to Tarsha that Tammy's colouring worked so well without it that she didn't need to mess around for hours with that stuff.

Aha, but her bra strap was showing, he saw. Her very *tired-looking* bra strap. Minus hundreds of points for that. It was the wrong colour, too—beige, instead of blue or black, slipping across the top of her shoulder beyond the neckline of her clingy dress.

Oh, damn it, forget the bra strap! She had such delicate, beautiful skin...

'You look lovely,' Laird told her sincerely, but his eyes must have arrowed unconsciously to the bra strap, in a final useless attempt to be sensible about the woman, because she looked down at it and fingered it, and a look of horror appeared on her face.

'It's the wrong one,' she said. 'Help! I forgot to change it to the black one. Oh, I have to go back up!'

'Tammy, it's all right. Really. You look—'

'No, it isn't!'

In a flurry of haste she hooked her index finger into the back of each shoe to lever them off, dropped them at the bottom of the stairs and darted up in her stockinged feet, leaving Laird feeling terrible that he'd channelled Tarsha enough to notice the bra and hadn't masked his reaction to it.

'You looked fine before,' he said, as soon as she appeared again. 'Really. You looked great.'

'No, I didn't. I bounced.' For a moment her hands flattened over those two generous, rounded shapes, then she dropped them again, as if realising that a woman wasn't supposed to touch her own breasts in front of a man.

Laird experienced a sudden and very primal shock to the groin. She bounced in the other bra. And he'd missed it. But she'd just touched the palms of her hands to the soft fabric that clothed those lovely breasts and he hadn't missed that. The gesture had drawn his gaze there like a magnet. He had to suppress a groan of regret and need— almost of pain.

She bounced.

Never mind. He hadn't missed it after all, as it turned out. She said goodbye and goodnight to the kids and her mother, gave a couple of last-minute instructions about the whereabouts of clean pyjamas, and then, as they went down her front steps, Laird discovered that she bounced in this bra as well, just the perfect amount.

He had to fight not to keep looking until she saw him doing it. Had to fight not to start picturing those generous, curvy, sexy breasts without the bra. Not to mention the rest of her, so smooth and ripe and generous beneath his hungry touch.

He began to feel thick-headed and punch-drunk and giddy. A satisfying warmth filled his veins—a mix of anticipation and desire and earthy contentment that, once again, he couldn't remember feeling in years.

Or ever?

Who else in his life had ever made him feel this way? Feet grounded, head in the stars.

'Thanks for this, Laird,' Tammy said beside him, just before they reached his car. 'It's a real treat to have a meal out without the kids. You'd better watch me. There's a serious risk I'll get up on the restaurant table, hitch up my dress and start dancing. You might have to grab my ankle and pull me to the floor.'

'I'm looking forward to it,' he said, matching her jokey tone.

But then he started thinking about her ankles, about running his hands up her smooth, curvy legs, to her thighs and beyond. His head felt even thicker, and if he felt this close to being drunk now, when he hadn't touched a drop, how would he feel after a glass or two of wine?

You never knew until you tried…

Yes, but the strength of this scared him.

## CHAPTER SIX

'DECIDED yet?' Laird asked.

Tammy hadn't. She still held the open menu in front of her, overwhelmed by choice. Overwhelmed by being here. Overwhelmed most of all by Laird, seated across from her, looking so...oh...*eligible*, or something. The kind of man who turned women's heads and made other men stand up straighter and square their jaws.

The last time she'd eaten in a restaurant that even approached this level of magnificence had been the night she'd told Tom about the ultrasound, five years ago.

He'd known she was pregnant, and that this one was hitting her harder. She'd told him of her intuition that something was different. Her doctor had scheduled her for an ultrasound at eight weeks to see what was going on, but it was her third pregnancy so she'd told Tom, 'Don't come.' His army routine was pretty tightly regulated. She would have more need for him to take time off from his duties later on, when the baby was born.

Babies, she'd discovered.

And she must have known at some level that he would react badly to the news because she'd said, 'Let's go out to eat, tonight,' and then had bided her time until after he'd had a beer or two...

Right. Make a decision, Tammy. Prawns or pasta or that lamb thing or the fish, or even the duck...Don't dither and keep him waiting.

'How many courses are you having?' she asked Laird cautiously.

'Starting with two. If I'm still hungry, I'll order dessert.' He dropped his voice a little. 'Don't hang back, will you, Tammy? I promise you, you won't eat an embarrassing amount more than I do.'

'Ooh, don't bet on that!'

He laughed.

For a moment or two she laughed back and felt fizzy and happy inside.

Then, not for the first time, a sudden aftershock of self-doubt kicked in, and she wondered if he was laughing *at* her or *with* her. Maybe she shouldn't have spoken so frankly about her appetite. Maybe she should pretend to be one of those women who picked at their food as if suffering from perpetual hunger would win them a gold medal.

She teetered on the edge of choosing a salad and a light chicken dish, then thought, Darn it, no, I'm going to order what I really want. There's no point in pretending to be who I'm not. I'd make a pretty bad job of it anyway!

But what was it that she really wanted? Finally, she made a decision, and then heard Laird order exactly the two dishes that had run a close second in her choice.

'Ooh,' she said again.

'Problem?'

'I'd been thinking about the duck, too.' Then she added, before she thought, 'Could we swap tastes?'

'You'd do that?' He laughed again. 'At a place like this?'

He'd brought her to the best restaurant at the casino, in Melbourne's Southbank district. Just outside, marching in a row along the pedestrian walkway, a symphony of gas flames flared dramatically at regular intervals, making passing tourists and even locals pause and point and gasp, and at their window-side table Tammy and Laird could both feel the radiant heat every time the jets went off.

Which was not what made her flush.

'Oh. N-no,' she stammered. 'Not if you don't want to. I'm sorry, I'm used to—'

'It's fine.'

'Eating half-finished chicken nuggets off my kids' plates. I shouldn't even—'

'It's *fine*, Tammy.'

'Be at a place like this. It'll cost more than my food budget for a week. And people would stare, wouldn't they, if we were—'

'I almost ordered the lamb myself. I'd love a share of yours.'

'Passing our plates back and forth.'

'And I don't give a damn what "people" think, Tammy. There are enough kinds of tyranny in our lives as it is, without that. Don't you think?'

She finally calmed down enough to take in what he'd said. He was watching her in that way he had been doing lately. Sort of thoughtful and a little bemused, as if he'd found himself in a parallel universe and couldn't work out how and why it was different from the usual one, let alone what he was doing in it.

Sometimes she felt the same way.

'Tyranny,' she said, enjoying the taste of the word on her tongue, because it was Laird who had just used it.

'You think that's too strong?'

'What kinds of tyranny?'

'Time, money, rules and protocol, all sorts of things.'

'You're right. I've never used the word tyranny in that sense but, yes.'

'What tyrannies do you suffer under?'

'Oh, let me think…'

It was one of those rambling, odd conversations that went in so many directions you couldn't remember where it had begun. Laird seemed to forget his bemusement, and Tammy forgot that he was spending her whole week's family food budget taking her out to a single meal. They swapped plates twice with each course, and if anyone was staring at such gauche, terrible behaviour, Tammy didn't notice because she was too busy looking at Laird and the plates, and laughing at something he'd said.

She lost track of time. Often, she caught Laird looking at her when he thought she wouldn't see, and she knew, just knew, that she was looking at him the same way, even though she tried not to—with a quality of disbelief and wonder, as well as a very healthy dose of desire.

What is happening here? This is magical and crazy and I must be reading it all wrong. I must be out of my head and Laird is definitely out of his! she thought.

This was the kind of place where dinner took two hours, and you enjoyed every minute. The waiter brought dessert menus, catapulting Tammy into a should-I-or-shouldn't-I conflict with which she was very familiar. She had a pretty good idea of the outcome, too.

It would involve chocolate.

But then her mobile rang and she heard Mum's voice.

'I'm sorry to be doing this. They've caught some kind of tummy bug, love.'

'Have I been gone that long?' she said blankly.

'They were suspiciously quiet from the moment you walked out the door. Three of them so far—Sarah, Lachlan and Lucy. They didn't eat dinner and at first I thought they were just tired, but then Sarah said she felt sick. Don't hurry home, because I'm managing, but Lucy's pretty miserable, poor sweetheart, and she's asking for you. She's already vomited twice.'

Mum had been known to send mixed signals on occasion, just like Tammy herself. Faced with a choice between 'Don't hurry home,' and 'Lucy's pretty miserable,' what could a good mother do?

'I think we'll have to skip dessert, Laird...' she told him, her voice slowing with regret.

'Problem at home?'

'Stomach upset. Oh, I hope you don't catch it! You were right in the thick of the germs tonight!'

'What about you?'

'Oh, there's little doubt I'll get it, if it's infectious. But I'm off until Monday.'

'So you'll spend your precious free time feeling like death warmed up and battling to be fit for work.'

She shrugged, acknowledging that he was right. She was used to it. Kind of.

He looked at her in silence for a long moment, until she began to wonder if he was angry, or if he was going to insist they stay for dessert, but then he said, 'What can I do, Tammy? How can I help? I mean it. There must be something. Concrete, practical help. That's what you need, isn't it?'

'We'll be fine. Kids bounce back fast. You're used to the ill, frail ones, but my lot are pretty healthy. I was very lucky, I carried the triplets through to thirty-two weeks. Ben had a few problems, especially with his eyes, but they're fine now.'

'Are you changing the subject?'

'I think I'd just like to get home. This has been the most fabulous meal, thank you.'

'It has, it's been great. But, yes, if you want to get home to the kids…' After that, he went quiet. Slid his credit card into the bill folder, then signed the slip. Hooked her bag strap off the back of the chair where she'd hung it and passed it to her. All of it accompanied by just a few superficial words.

Outside the restaurant, in the casino foyer, he stopped her in a quiet corner.

'Hang on a minute, don't be in such a rush.' Hand on her shoulder. Other hand pivoting her to face him. 'There's one more thing we have to take care of first.'

She froze, with her heart beating fast. He didn't have to kiss her. She didn't expect that kind of gallant finishing touch. Oh, lord, how could she let him know, tactfully, that he was off the hook, that kissing wasn't required, and save them both from this unnecessary embarrassment? Why had his eyes gone so dark? She loved the grey hue of them in daylight, too, but this was…this was…oh.

'I thought I'd have a better chance to lead up to this,' he said, and she barely heard him over the pounding in her ears and the flustered whirl of her thoughts. 'But you're in a hurry to get home, and the moment I'm parked in front of your house you'll leap out of the car, I know you will, and I'll have lost the chance.'

'I'm—'

'You probably won't even let me inside in case I catch something. So it's now or never.' His hands massaged her shoulders with a light, caressing touch. His voice dropped to a husky whisper. She could feel the heat and brush of his thighs through her dress. 'And I'm not that interested in never.'

'Laird, I don't—You don't—'

'Shh... Come on, stop...' He pressed his finger against her lips.

Then he pressed his mouth there.

Even though she'd known it was about to happen, it still took her by surprise. The heat of it. The sweetness. The surging need.

Oh, in both of them.

She needed this. Just this one kiss. Please. Now. In case no man ever kissed her again.

No, in case Laird Burchell never kissed her again.

She wrapped her arms around his shoulders, not even thinking to hold back, or make him wait, or leave him in any doubt about her response. She parted her lips and tasted him, and he took his cue to go deeper, flooding her whole body with sensation and desire, just with the way his lips moved.

The fruit and spice of red wine mingled in their mouths.

The light roughness of his cheek brushed against hers. Her breasts pressed into him, and her nipples went hard and tight. Her heart beat even faster.

She just wanted to hold him and forget everything but this. She closed her eyes, giving herself up to pure sensation, already knowing that she was like putty in his hands—the hands that were running over her back, whispering against the fabric of her dress, pulling on the skirt. She was so bad at hiding how she felt. He'd know. He'd understand exactly what this was doing to her.

Oh, she had to stop. Mum was waiting for her. The kids needed her.

And she was giving way too much to this man, when he couldn't possibly want it—when he'd kissed her because that's just what you do, the two of you, a man and a woman, when you've been out and had some wine.

What was that horrible expression? Beer goggles. Almost any woman could look temporarily attractive to a man if the timing and the lighting and the amount of alcohol were right.

She had five kids, she had no money, she had a badly wounded and mistrustful heart, she had—

He'd let her go. He'd stopped. She felt the easing away of his weight and strength, the loss of his mouth. Her own lips already felt swollen, and her breathing had gone short and uneven. Opening her eyes, she found him still just inches away, his hands forming into fists at his sides.

'Sorry,' he said. 'That didn't happen quite how I planned it.'

'Oh…um…'

'You're a hard woman to stop kissing, Tammy Prunty.'

Horrified, she backed away. So it had all come from her!

She'd held him so tight, she'd devoured him with her mouth because he felt so good. He'd been too polite to try to—

But he was laughing, bemused again.

'Hey, I'm saying I liked it,' he told her softly, brushing his knuckles lightly along her jaw. 'Don't you realise that? I really, really liked it. I *loved* it, and I couldn't let you go. But we're in a public place, even though there's no one much around. Don't want to get arrested for lewd behaviour on our first date.'

'Mmm, could be sensible to leave that until the next one,' she managed to say, then heard the echo of her own words in her head and realised that she'd only dug herself in deeper. Did he have the slightest intention of there being a 'next one'?

'Sounds great.' His eyes and voice teased. 'Somehow I'm seeing a fountain and splashing limbs next time. Smudged make-up.'

'Mussed-up hair,' she offered, thinking of her fingers running through those short dark strands of his.

'Exactly. Discarded piles of clothing. Chocolate body paint. Disorderly conduct. That kind of thing. Are we on the same page?'

'Um, yes… No… I hope so, I hope we are.' She was laughing helplessly. Her blood sang. Her brain clanged with warning bells. She didn't trust this, or him, or herself, and wanted to laugh about all of it. Or cry. 'I have no idea. I— I—You—We—You'd better take me home,' she finished, because it was the only sensible thing she could say.


The kids were better by Sunday night, and miraculously neither Tammy nor her mother contracted the bug at all.

Tammy was gripped by a raging virulence of a different kind. She went around in a daze all weekend. It felt the way her first kiss had felt at fourteen. The memory cascaded through her whole body at the tiniest trigger.

At the sound of Laird's voice when he phoned on Saturday to see how she and the kids were faring. At the smell of the dress she'd worn to the restaurant, when she brought it out of her wardrobe to check in daylight if it was still clean. At the taste of the glasses of red wine her mother poured for each of them on Saturday night, after they'd washed load after load of soiled sheets and clothes, and cleaned up the worst of the mess.

'We've earned this!' Mum said.

While Tammy thought hotly, *He kissed me.*

And he'd done it as if he'd liked it and wanted more, as if it had been the liqueur cherry on top of a big chocolate dessert, piled high with whipped cream.

Or had she read him all wrong?

*I can't be fourteen again. It's dangerous. It's frightening. It's doomed. And I don't have time!*

On Monday afternoon, Tammy came home from a day shift to find the house tidier and more sparkling clean than she'd seen it in years. 'He sent a cleaning team,' her mother explained in a helpless tone, when Tammy reached her in the kitchen, ready to yell at her for working too hard. 'That Dr Burchell of yours, I mean.'

'Mum! I thought you must have done it.'

'I couldn't possibly have, in one afternoon.'

'How did *they*?'

'They arrived at one o'clock, three of them, and stayed until four. They said it was paid for and organised. They showed me the invoice and told me who'd done it, and it was him. That doctor of yours.'

'He's not mine.'

'Love, three hours of professional cleaners!'

'He feels sorry for me, that's all. He—he's being nice. It's not all that hard to be nice when you have plenty of money.'

'Tammy, you're sounding angry.'

*At myself. For wanting to cry about this. For wanting to read way too much into it. For knowing it's going to go round and round in my thoughts for days.*

'I'm not angry. I'm just— I thought he was looking at me sideways a bit today. Only saw him on the hop, but the way he smiled, as if he had a really nice secret…' She shook her head, as helpless as Mum.

Mum was looking at her, and seeing too much.

Tammy burst into rapid speech. 'I just don't want to assume it's significant. We went out once. We talked all the way through the meal, and—and swapped tastes of what we'd ordered. And laughed a fair bit. It was nice, but… A man like him, Mum…'

'What, and you have nothing to offer? My fabulous daughter?'

'*What* do I have to offer? What?' She spread her hands, then dropped them. 'Now you're the one looking angry!'

'Stop me before I say something about a certain person stripping your confidence to the bone.'

Tom.

Neither of them needed to say his name.

'This isn't about him,' Tammy said.

'It isn't? Of course it is!'

'I'm being realistic, that's all.'

'What do you have to offer? You have everything to offer! You're bright, funny, warm, giving, hard-working, a wonderful down-to-earth mother...'

'I have a daunting, impossible number of young children. I'm at least seven kilos overweight, and that's being kind to myself. I pinch pennies until I start to feel as if I'm pinching myself, as if my mouth is pinching tight, like a tight little purse pinched in a pair of cramped, obsessive hands...'

'So you deserve someone who'll send in a cleaning team after your kids have a stomach bug. You should see the bathrooms, Tammy. You should *smell* the bathrooms! I don't know what products they used, but the smell is heavenly. Like daphne, or gardenia.'

'Really?' The anticipation of the scent in her nostrils dragged Tammy temporarily up out of her doubts. 'I must go and look before bathtime messes it all up. It's—it's wonderful, isn't it?'

She looked around. The light fittings were free of dust. The cork floor in the kitchen gleamed. The film of grease on the ceiling above the stove, where she never had time to climb up to clean, was gone.

'Oh, sheesh, they even did the windows!' she realised out loud. 'I could put my hand through them if I didn't know they were there.'

'You should send him a card,' Mum said. Too innocently. 'I have some nice ones in my desk, blank, so you can write your own message. I'll find them, and you can choose.'

So Tammy sat in her bedroom that night like a fourteen-year-old writing secrets in her diary. She waited until after the kids were asleep, and struggled over the wording on a piece of scrap paper, not daring to think that she'd get it right the first time.

'Dear Laird, thank you so much for sending the cleaners.'

'Dear Laird, you didn't have to do it, but it made my week!'

Dear Laird, please don't ever do anything like that ever again, because I'm pretty tough and I can stand life's struggles, with Mum's help. It's kindness that I can't take, and can't trust, after Tom. It's wondering how much you meant by it, if it was just a throw-away gesture, or if it came from the heart. It's thinking I could get very quickly used to being spoiled that way, and then it would be so, so hard when the spoiling stopped.

'All the best, Tammy.'

'Hugs, Tammy.'

'Love, Tammy.'

No, I can't use that word, can I? The L word? It's way too loaded and scary, even thrown away on a signature line. I don't love you. Of course I don't. But I'm scared that I could, if you made it too easy for me, and then where would I be?

Writing the card, all sixty-four words, took her over an hour.

Laird felt like a child awaiting the reaction to a hand-made Christmas gift. Would she like it? Did she like it? Didn't she love it? How could she not?

On Friday night, he'd dropped Tammy home and obeyed her strict order not to enter the house. 'It'll be awful, Laird, and you'll catch something. You don't have your resistance built up by years of pre-school. I'm not letting you near the front door.' At home, he'd tried to catch up on some medical reading but the words had just blurred.

And then he hadn't been able to sleep.

He knew Tammy wouldn't be asleep either. She'd be in and out of children's rooms all night, soothing miserable tears, changing messy pyjamas, being strong and cheerful even when she was dropping in her tracks.

The offer of help he'd made at the restaurant...ridiculous. Was he intending to follow her children around with a mop and bucket? Send in a pizza delivery when their stomachs were still in rebellion?

Then he'd thought, *Cleaners!* and it seemed perfect. A genuine way to help. Not too intrusive. Not too personal. A kindness, rather than the grand-piano-sized, exhilarating gesture of...oh, what could you call it...just *wowiness* that he really felt like making.

Wow, Tammy.

The way you kissed me. The way the restaurant lighting shone on your hair. The way you laughed every time those gas jets went off and we saw the flames billowing up into the night and felt the heat. The way you juggled those plates back and forth.

Your breasts.

Bouncing.

Making you embarrassed because you were wearing the wrong bra.

I loved the feel of you in my hands, all that silky, scented fabric and skin, so soft and curvy and giving...so giving.

She didn't think to hold herself back. There was no illusion of sophistication to mask her carefully concealed self-doubts. Tammy's self-doubts dangled from her sleeve, her kisses weren't a performance at all, and her reaction to him hiring the cleaners wouldn't be a performance either.

Brittany, the strongest of the surviving two Vitelli triplets, was going home today, and Tammy was helping Alison to prepare for her discharge. The little girl was still on oxygen and would need frequent check-ups to look at her heart, her lungs, her eyes and her general development, but she'd begun to feed well and was putting on weight daily.

Consulting about another tiny patient nearby with a paediatric heart surgeon he'd called in, Laird couldn't help listening to every word.

'I'm so nervous,' Alison said. A friend had spirited her off to the hair salon yesterday and she looked better, fresher, with those dark roots gone. She'd begun to take care of herself just a little bit better, which gave Laird confidence that she'd take care of Brittany and still manage to come in to see Harry.

Tammy gave her shoulder a squeeze. 'Good! I'd be worried if you weren't,' she said calmly, as she completed some notes.

'I couldn't eat breakfast.'

'Nature's way of telling you that it's totally daunting to be taking a premmie home from hospital for the first time. But it's not a one-way street, Alison. If you need to, if you have any doubts or concerns at all, you'll bring her back.'

'Oh, I hope not! Oh, I so don't want to have to do that!'

'Of course not, and that's why you're going to tell me right now if there's the tiniest thing you don't understand about the oxygen equipment, or anything else. You have no smokers in your house, right? None who make regular visits?'

'No, thank goodness. If we did, I'd send them outside.'

'You have the phone number of the NICU on speed dial.'

'I have a reliable thermometer, I have frozen breast milk for if she's too tired to suck.'

'Harry's going to need more of the frozen milk soon. Dr Burchell upped him to ten mils this morning.'

'Oh…see? I hadn't caught up with that. I'm so busy thinking about Brittany. How are we going to manage, with one baby here and one at home?'

'What help do you have at home?'

'Mum's coming again tomorrow, staying for six weeks and longer if we need her to. She's very keen to help, but she says she's forgotten everything she ever knew about babies.'

'Good,' Tammy told her firmly. 'That's what you want. The ones who think they remember it all are the dangerous ones. You don't want her slipping three tablespoons of port wine into Brittany's bottle because that's what mothers did when you were a baby.'

Alison looked appalled for a second, then realised that Tammy was joking. The wicked look in those blue eyes gave it away. Laird could have told her that.

'Seriously, though,' Tammy said, 'it sounds as if she's willing to learn about Brittany's needs, and that's good.'

'She'll be good with Harry, too. We named him after Dad…' Alison grew tearful and Tammy hugged her. Laird resolutely moved his head thirty degrees so that the two women and the baby no longer featured in his peripheral vision.

'Unusual defect, so I'm bringing in Michael Begley from Royal Victoria, and I'm thinking we'll do it tomorrow,' he heard. 'Provided you think she's strong enough.'

He snapped into focus quickly, put Tammy out of his

mind for the moment and told the other man, 'That's sooner than I'd envisaged. I'd like to get this little girl's weight up another couple of hundred grams first.'

'Is she putting on weight? With her heart working this hard?'

'She is. It's slow, but she's a fighter. Look, if it seems like she's not progressing, we'll have to rethink. Is Begley available over the next two or three weeks?'

'I'll have to check. I know he's away in the second half of November.'

'You wouldn't feel confident tackling this without him?' They'd looked at the test results and scans together. Like most surgeons, Eric Van was energised by the prospect of tackling something new, but he wasn't the kind of man to overestimate his own abilities.

'Confident, yes, eager, no,' he said. 'If I can say to the parents, look, this is a very rare defect, but we have a surgeon coming in who's seen a very similar problem before…'

'Makes sense,' Laird said. 'So our job is to get her strong enough before mid-November.'

'That's how I see it, yes.'

Half an hour later, Laird found the card from Tammy in his pigeonhole. It was a nice card, in an aqua envelope labeled *Laird*, showing a tranquil tropical beach scene. He flipped it open.

'Dear Laird, thank you so much for smoothing out my week in such a wonderful way! Mum was bowled over, and so was I. You didn't have to! Please don't do it again! But I'm so grateful for your doing it this once. Every time I go into the bathroom or look through those sparkly windows, my spirits lift. Once again, thank you, Tammy.'

He found her in the break room, gulping a cup of tea and a milk arrowroot biscuit far too fast. She'd let down her hair in order to redo it—it often worked too loose during the day—and she had the stretchy piece of black elastic around her wrist ready for the tightly scraped ponytail she would make once she'd gulped the last of her tea.

Laird wanted to yell at her, and he must have projected the fact in his body language, because her blue eyes went wide and she put the tea down on the countertop with a bump. She opened her mouth to speak—her lower lip glistened enticingly from the tea—but he didn't give her time.

'I didn't want you to write a bloody card about it,' he said.

He knew he was coming on too strong, but...hell! He'd kissed her on Friday night and he knew she'd reacted exactly the same way he had—wanting more, shocked at the intensity of one semi-public kiss—but she kept wilfully misunderstanding what that meant, what *he* meant, and what he wanted.

Well, what did he want? asked the treacherous part of him that channelled Tarsha's well-meant opinion.

Oh, hell, he couldn't ask himself those questions now!

Tammy lifted her chin, and lifted her shoulders, making those delicious breasts push more firmly against the bland fabric of her surgical blues. 'It's good manners, isn't it? I wanted to say thank you.'

'So you should have said thank you. Not written it on a pretty card. Not in that dismissive way.'

'Dismissive?'

'Distancing. So polite. And brittle. It wasn't *you*, Tammy.'

'You're such an authority on me?'

'I think so,' he said quietly, stepping closer. He wanted

to touch her, but wasn't yet in reach, and anyway this was the break room. Nurses or parents or visitors looking for a glass of water could show up at any moment. He kept his voice low. 'I'd like to be an authority on you. I like everything I know about you so far.'

'Except the fact that I write polite thank-you cards,' she reminded him. She folded her arms across her chest, the defensive pose belying the hectic pink in her cheeks. He loved that pink. It told him a lot.

'Except that one specific polite thank-you card,' he corrected her. 'You do it on purpose, this way you misunderstand me. You're talking about good manners—you used them like a shield with that card, Tammy. The manners, the misunderstanding. They're both shields. Deliberate shields. That wasn't a one-off, the other—'

'I don't want you to keep sending cleaners,' she cut in. 'Or any other kind of favour. I just don't.' She waved her hands at him for a moment, then pressed them against her hot cheeks.

'I don't mean the cleaners, you crazy person, I mean dinner, I mean spending time with you, taking you out to the vineyard with the kids, spoiling you a bit.'

His hands itched to touch her—to push that wild, bright hair back from her neck so he could kiss her there. He wanted to cool her cheeks with the brush of his mouth and breath, wanted to hug her until she laughed and fought for air, wanted to whisper in her ear a long, sinful list of all the ways he desired her.

'It seems like charity,' she finished, the words so far from where his thoughts had travelled that he almost didn't understand them.

'Taking you to dinner?'

'Sending cleaners. I'm not the kind of woman you should be going out with, Laird. I'm just not.'

'So tell me what kind of a woman is that?'

'Someone thin and single and gorgeous,' she listed so fast he barely caught the words.

'Sending cleaners brings us to this?'

'Yes, because a single, gorgeous, childless woman wouldn't need a cleaner. She'd have one, or she'd clean her own place in half an hour a week, because single women on their own don't get things dirty.'

'Can we please not talk about the damned cleaners any more? Let alone about this single, childless woman of yours who doesn't exist. I'm trying to ask you out again!'

'Even though you're yelling at me'

'Yes!'

'Why do you want to go out with me again?'

'Because you make me crazy. In all sorts of ways.'

'And that's how it works? A woman makes a man crazy, so he asks her out?'

'Sometimes, yes.' His voice rose again, despite his attempts to stay low key and in control. 'Don't you know that?' Oh, lord, this was frustrating! 'Sometimes that's exactly how it bloody works!'

# CHAPTER SEVEN

'I WANT to have dinner with you again,' Laird said, visibly attempting to curb his impatience. 'This time, when your kids hopefully won't get sick—poor little munchkins, I do know it wasn't their fault!—so we don't have to rush you home. Just a simple dinner, focused on the two of us, no distractions. Is that too much to ask?'

'I'm sorry about the other night,' Tammy answered, struggling to get past the fact that he was almost yelling at her, that he'd hated her card, and yet he still apparently, for some mystifying reason, wanted to see her again.

Was he right when he'd said just now that a man and a woman making each other crazy could be the most telling indication of what they felt?

She wanted to see him again, too, but that was a lot easier to understand, and a lot scarier.

Fight this just a little bit, Tammy Prunty!

'So…when?' he demanded.

'I can't just do dinner,' she said, instead of what she wanted to say, which was, *Yes, yes, yes.*

'Not just dinner? What do you mean?'

'It's not fair to Mum. It's so hard to persuade her to take time for herself.'

'Now, why does that sound familiar, I wonder?' he muttered.

'I know. I'm the same. I do realise that. But they're my kids. I'm the one who should be driving myself into the ground, not my sixty-two-year-old widowed mother.' She took a deep breath. 'I want to see you...' Having said it, she immediately felt three times as vulnerable, yet managed to stay firm, on one point at least. 'But dinner has to be the reward at the end. If we're going to do something together, it has to be a day out somewhere with the kids, so Mum has the whole place to herself for a while, and dinner and having her babysit for us comes afterwards.'

It was a test.

Laird probably recognised the fact as clearly as she did.

If he wasn't willing to stump up enough of his free time to spend a few hours with her children, getting to know them...*putting up with them*, as would no doubt be involved for at least some of the time, as they were normal human children, not angels...then she needed to say no to dinner and put a stop, right now, to the frivolous, impossible idea that this craziness between them might go somewhere or mean something.

'Where shall we take them?' he said. Bravely.

Without hesitation, Tammy replied, 'The zoo.'

The zoo was always...well...a zoo. Five very individual children did not all like the same animals, or like them to the same degree.

Ben was a total animal nut, but with a four-year-old's tendency to live in the present, he couldn't envisage that if he loved looking intently at the elephants for fifteen minutes, he'd probably love looking intently at the giraffes and monkeys just as much. He had to be dragged and cajoled and bribed from one viewing area to the next, while Lachlan was the exact opposite and ran from enclosure to walkway to viewing platform and would have covered the whole place in half an hour and been ready to go home, if the other kids hadn't slowed him down.

Meanwhile, Laura and Lucy only liked cute animals. Kittens. Ponies. Sarah had begun to develop a certain age-appropriate interest in ponies also, but had a warm enthusiasm for creepy animals as well, preferably the kind without legs.

Tammy, meanwhile, had no tastes or preferences whatsoever. Mothers of large families learned not to, because it only complicated things further. She just wanted there to be no fighting between them all.

And once you factored in snacks, and lunch, and water bottles, and hats, and sunscreen, and tired legs, and the issue of whether she should take the now-battered double-seater pram, which two triplets at a time just managed to still fit into...

'If you're serious,' she told Laird, 'I'd suggest the zoo.'

'This is not just a test, is it?' he said, indicating that he'd indeed read her mind a minute ago. The light in his grey eyes was both exasperated and amused. 'It's a gruelling six-hour exam!'

They arranged it for the following Saturday.

The weather forecast co-operated with a prediction of full sunshine, although this meant it might get uncomfortably hot for several hours in the middle of the day. Laird arranged to drive to Tammy's, from where they would proceed to the zoo in her battered second-hand seven-seater minivan—for which she didn't apologise, because she'd gained a firmer grip on herself now, thanks to mental pep talks for several days. As Laird had divined, this was a very serious, very important exam, and if he couldn't deal with the humble nature of her minivan, then he wasn't going to score a passing grade.

Hmm. No sense making the whole thing too tough on an otherwise promising student, however.

After lying awake in the night, worrying about the strong possibility of there being empty muesli bar packets and old notes from school lying crumpled on the minivan floor, Tammy got up at six and cleaned the whole thing before any of the kids woke up.

Although the disappearance of camouflaging dirt did then serve to emphasise the scuffed seating and exterior dents and scrapes, the debris-free floor and polished chrome and glass were nonetheless an improvement.

At the zoo, the seven of them felt like a family.

While she often earned stares from strangers when out with the kids on her own—what was any woman doing by herself in public with such a large family?—the looks she received today were significantly more smile-laden and forgiving. What cute triplets! What a distinguished-looking dad they had! And look at the way he kept abreast of Lachlan's impatient whirl from zebras to wombats to snakes, and steered him cheerfully back to Tammy and the others! Distinguished *and* hands on.

'Should I try and rope him in more firmly?' he asked her at one point, not as if Lachlan was being a brat but as if Laird himself scrupulously wanted to do the right thing.

'It's tough,' Tammy answered. 'He's a good little lad, but he's just not as interested in creatures as the other four. He's more of a building and engineering type. I went with the majority preference, so he's the one who's hard done by.'

'How about we go for a carousel ride? Would he like that?'

'They'd all love it.'

'You, too?' He grinned at her.

'There have to be a few perks for being a parent! Yes, I'll have a ride.'

So they all did, even Laird. The triplets were old enough now to have a horse each, as long as Tammy rode her own wooden mount close by. The children were grinning and laughing, which made her grin, too, sharing their pleasure.

'You were joking about the perks,' Laird told her when they stepped down from the ride, all feeling a little dizzy. 'But you're right. It is a perk. Recapturing the innocence, or something. I hadn't realised how good that would feel.'

'Recapturing the wonder,' she suggested.

He nodded. 'That's it. The wonder. Hmm, and the nausea, too. Woo, I think my stomach must be empty.'

They ate a sandwich lunch bought from one of the zoo kiosks and juggled the children's wants and needs successfully until after four o'clock. The reptiles for Sarah, the animal nursery for Laura and Lucy, the scientific details Ben needed about every creature they saw, and the running around that Lachlan wanted to do. On the way home, all three triplets were tired enough to sleep in the car.

Laird had made a dinner booking for seven o'clock, and Tammy thought he'd go off and grab a couple of hours of breathing space and sanity before he picked her up again, but he insisted on coming into the house.

'I have to get dinner organised for Mum,' she warned him bluntly, because if he imagined the two of them sitting on the back veranda, sipping cool drinks with little paper umbrellas in them for the next hour, he was very wrong.

'So I'm on entertainment duty?'

'You could go home. Or you could cheat, and put on a DVD.'

'Might be able to come up with something better than that.'

'You don't actually have to stay, though, Laird, I mean it.'

'I have a change of clothing in the car,' he drawled. 'I was a Scout once, I'm prepared.'

Helplessly, she said, 'OK, if you're that much of a sucker for punishment,' and turned her attention to making chicken casserole and spaghetti sauce—a double batch of each so that she would end up with a meal for tonight and three more frozen for the future. In the background, she heard the kids' voices and Laird's, and when she went to see what they were doing, she discovered they were building a zoo.

'Isn't it fantastic, Mummy?' Sarah yelped excitedly.

It was.

Lachlan tackled the construction, using wooden and plastic blocks, a blue teatowel and a green handkerchief for water areas, even wooden train tracks for a miniature zoo railway. Ben grouped the animals thematically. 'We can't have lions in with kangaroos, Lucy! Lions are carnivorous!' Sarah was the head keeper for the reptiles and nocturnal animals. Laird supervised the whole thing, settled disputes, threw in creative suggestions, and probably got more of a physical workout, crawling around on the carpet, than he'd expected.

'Show-off,' Tammy said to him, because it unsettled her that he was being so good about this. How long since she'd had an energetic, willing, intelligent man in the house to play with her kids? How long before the novelty factor would wear off for him?

'Next you're going to remind me that it all has to be cleaned up properly if I want dessert.'

'That's right.'

'Someone'll cry,' he warned. He had the sleeves of his light cotton sweater pushed up and several blocks in his hand. He looked strong and relaxed and more like an athlete than a doctor. Tammy had to hide the way her heart flipped at the sight of him.

'And I don't want it to be me,' she said, mock-sternly, 'coming home at ten-thirty tonight to find all of this littered on the floor, or Mum on her hands and knees, tidying up.'

'You're not really angry, are you?'

'No,' she admitted. 'I'm teasing.'

'And do you really want it tidied up?'

She sighed. 'I do. But how can I be that much of a dragon, when it's so spectacular?'

'I have to admit, though, it's right in the middle of the carpet. We didn't survey our site very well. Someone'll trip over it.'

'I'll see what Mum wants when she comes in.'

Tammy went back to the kitchen to finish her cooking, but at six-thirty when the children's dinner was served and Mum had done her usual rap at the back door—'It's just Grandma!'—the zoo had been carefully transplanted to the edges of the living room, to leave a clear space in the middle of the carpet and an impression of satisfactory order rather than undisciplined chaos.

'You'd better change,' Laird said. 'Can't go to a Thai restaurant smelling like spaghetti.'

That night there was no emergency phone call from Mum. They lingered over a meal fragrant with lemon grass and coriander and chilli until almost ten o'clock, and still Tammy didn't want to go home.

'But we must,' she said, convincing herself more than him.

A glass and a half of white wine had softened everything around the edges, including her never-very-impressive ability to hide her feelings. Oh, she was having such a nice time tonight! They'd talked non-stop. He kept making her laugh, and when she said something funny herself, he laughed, too. A lot of men didn't think funny meant sexy when it came to women, but Laird apparently did.

'Mum won't go to bed until I'm back,' she went on, 'even though her flat's only thirty metres away from the house, across a piece of lawn.'

At home, after Laird had insisted he would see Tammy inside and say thanks and goodnight to her mother, all was quiet. Five kids asleep, Mum beginning to doze on the couch, with the TV sound turned low. She yawned as she promised Tammy that no one had given any trouble. They'd all been hungry, they'd all cleaned their teeth. Even Sarah, the latest up, had been asleep by eight-thirty.

'Goodnight, love.' In the kitchen, by the back door, she hugged Tammy and kissed her on the cheek, then gave off an even more massive and this time transparently faked yawn, which Tammy just *knew* was intended as a subtle hint and reassurance.

If Laird happened to stay for coffee, and the coffee happened to get a little more intimate after a while, Mum would already be tactfully fast asleep.

*Thanks, Mum. I love you, too.*

She found Laird on his knees in the living-room, making some improvements to the zoo. He laughed when she caught him at it, and climbed to his feet. 'Sprung! I never totally grew up, did I?'

'You really are a show-off,' she told him.

'I'm a perfectionist. The primate enclosure was too small.'

'This is what you're going to do at your vineyard, isn't it? Play around with it until it's perfect. I bet the trees will look spectacular.'

'Come and see them. They're all planted—straight, this time—although I'm planning to order a couple more truck-loads. Bring the kids.'

'It sounds nice. I—I don't know.'

'Yes, you do.'

There was a moment of awkward silence while they smiled at each other in a goofy kind of way.

'So, did you want coffee?' she asked him.

'No, I thought we'd skip straight to the hard stuff.'

'Hard?'

'You. Hard to get. Let me kiss you properly tonight, Tammy…'

Before she could give him an answer, he'd taken charge, had switched in seconds from the relaxed type who was happy to crawl around the floor, playing zoos, to a man who knew what he wanted, wanted a heck of a lot and was totally accustomed to getting it.

He stepped in front of her and pushed her hair away

from her face. She'd left it loose tonight. Felt safer that way. At a pinch, her hair could screen a blush or a smile. It would shadow her face if she had to look down because she could no longer meet the light in his warm eyes. Laird liked her hair, and it apparently gave some people the illusion that she was pretty.

But now it betrayed her.

His fingers ran through it, releasing the scent of her shampoo all around them. Her scalp tingled and sent shivers all down her spine and across her skin. He bent and buried his face in the hard-to-tame waves, then kissed her neck, trailing his lips across her skin with slow, teasing intent. His breath felt hot. His touch sent up sparks. She shuddered and gasped, wrapping her arms around his body because she needed the support. She just *needed* him.

'I want you,' he said. 'There's something about you. Every inch of you. Your skin. The weight of your breasts in my hands. The way you smell. The way you laugh. The way you call me on things like my hobby vineyard and my pretty new trees.'

'But I'd love to see them.'

'You will. Soon. As soon as we can manage it. You're *real*, Tammy Prunty. I don't think I've ever met a woman as real as you.'

'I want you, too. So much. Sometimes I can't breathe. Or blink. Or speak. Or believe it's happening. Or—or think that this is really me. That this is happening to *me*.' The words spilled out on their own, and she cursed her own honesty.

A little restraint, Tammy, for once?

She couldn't.

She wasn't made that way.

His body felt so hard and warm and wonderful. He smelled right. Familiar and delicious, but new, too. She breathed him in, felt herself surrounded by his fresh male scent and it lit up something inside her that she'd forgotten or maybe had never known. His thighs brushed against her, his chest was like a wall, and she felt utterly safe with his strength, even on such new ground.

'What are we going to do about it?' he muttered.

She didn't answer, just lifted her face in search of his kiss. Their mouths crushed together, breathless and hungry, too impatient to be gentle or tender. It was a huge kiss, deep and almost bruising. Her body throbbed and ached and tingled and sang as she tasted him.

He had his hands in her hair again, lifting it off her neck, stroking her skin and curling the strands around his fingers. She arched her back, pressing her breasts against him so that he'd know what he'd done to her, shameless about it. Her nipples were hard and tight and tender.

She felt his hardness, too—the unique maleness of it nudging her body, betraying his need. He moved his hands to her breasts, cupping and lifting them so he could kiss the swollen slopes that rose above the dipping neckline of her shimmery, thin-strapped black top. She touched him everywhere she could reach, learning his body by heart, learning the way he responded, and all the different ways they fitted together.

How long since she'd done this? Or had wanted to do it?

A long time. Five years. Only days before Tom had moved out, when she'd still thought that they were just going through a temporary bad patch and soon they'd—

Stop, Tammy.

She didn't want to think about Tom.

But when she thought about Laird, she realised she was giving far too much, far too soon. What was her eagerness telling him? That she wanted to sleep with him tonight? That it would be easy, and without any serious implications?

It wouldn't.

Just thinking about it made her feel as if a big hand had reached into her stomach, taken a handful of her insides and twisted them into a knot. If she slept with him, she'd give him her heart.

At once.

Completely.

She knew herself well enough to be in no doubt of that. And her heart was so tender and sore. It was only the feeling of bruising and the fear of pain that allowed her to push him away.

Too gently. He didn't even understand what she was doing at first, and she had to say it in words. 'Can we stop?'

For several moments she felt him struggling against the demands of his body. He touched his fingertips to her lips and traced their shape while his hips and legs stayed pressed against her, making her fully aware of how aroused he was. 'Of course we can stop,' he said at last. 'But you have to tell me when you next have a day off with no night shift before it.'

'Um, next Saturday. I try to stay clear of too much weekend work.'

'So we'll go out to the vineyard with the kids then, give your mother some more time to herself.'

'Lachlan and Ben are going to a friend's place. It would just be the girls.'

'Whoever, as long as one of the girls is you. Want to meet me out there? I'll give you directions, or I can pick you up.'

'Give me directions.'

'I'll see you during the week at the hospital.'

'Give me the directions now. It's—it's different at the hospital.' She trusted this whole sizzle and fire and intensity even less when they were there.

He nodded at her words. Maybe he felt the same. She found a pen and an old note from school and he wrote the directions on the back of it, with a clarity and detail that made her smile. There was something protective about it, and a subtext that said he really, really didn't want her to get lost.

She felt ridiculously cherished by directions such as 'Big tree on LEFT' and 'If you get to the turn-off to Laidlaw Mountain Road, you've gone too far'. He finished the whole thing off with his mobile phone number, his land-line number, and even his home email address, then gave her back the scrappy piece of paper as if giving her a bunch of flowers.

When he'd gone, she folded it carefully and put it in her bag as if it was precious, her vulnerability and doubt battling with the sizzling happiness and expectation in her heart.

# CHAPTER EIGHT

THEY had rain during the week and Tammy crossed her fingers for it to clear. She imagined Laird bravely pretending that muddy footprints in his house and bored, house-bound kids running and shrieking through the rooms didn't bother him a bit.

In the NICU, two babies graduated to the high dependency unit. One of them was Max Parry, which was very good news, although his brother would be here in the NICU for longer. Fran was still looking exhausted and Chris had a hard time persuading her to take the breaks she needed. He and Alison Vitelli's husband Steve ganged up together and sent Fran and Alison off to the hospital cafeteria whenever they could. They were both good fathers, although very different people, and they somehow managed to appreciate each other's different emotional styles.

Two more newborns arrived, both of whom looked like they would only need a comparatively short stay. Tammy and Laird encountered each other several times a day—bright points in an average week, little memory-making moments that she hugged to herself at night in bed and then worried about.

By Friday, the rain had cleared and the forecast for the weekend was breezy and fine. Laird phoned that evening to confirm that Tammy and the girls were still coming, and she gave him an expected arrival time. 'I have to drop the boys off first.'

With the precious directions to the vineyard entrusted to Sarah in the minivan's front seat, Tammy left the city behind on Saturday. Suburban blocks gave way to acreage. There were hobby orchards beginning to fruit, shaggy family ponies standing in grassy paddocks, and they passed the garden centre where Laird had bought his trees.

Farther out, the farms and vineyards started. She turned 'LEFT' at the big tree, didn't make the dreaded mistake of going as far as Laidlaw Mountain Road, and found Laird's place, a modern log-cabin style house with wide verandas and huge, north-facing windows, set among a series of rolling slopes striped with rows of young vines, at the end of a long driveway. Behind the slopes rose the backdrop of the forested Dandenong Ranges.

Laird heard the van—well, its engine was pretty loud, due to the fact that it hadn't been running all that smoothly of late and she hadn't had the time or money to take it to the garage—and came out to meet them. 'No boys? That's right, you said. When do you need to pick them up?'

'They're staying the night with my friend Mel.'

'So you don't have a curfew.' He looked pleased.

Tammy wished he wouldn't do that.

The looking-pleased thing.

It drew her in, weakened her defences, gave her one of those giddy heart jumps that felt so scary and nice. She didn't know what he had planned for them today, and that was scary and nice, too—the thought of doing very little in the company of a man who made her blood sing and who took care of her and smiled at her and transparently planned to kiss her later on.

She saw his gaze settle on her mouth and stay there for too long, while he smiled. If he was already thinking about a kiss in delicious detail, so help her, so was she.

He was casually dressed in jeans and a cream and blue polo shirt, with those same clunky work boots he'd worn to the garden centre already crusted with dried mud. He must have washed his hair this morning, though, because it shone in the sun and she could smell the clean, fresh scent of soap and shampoo and sun-dried clothes.

Her own jeans and stretchy apricot cotton top actually felt a little less tight than they had the last time she'd worn them. She'd had a butterfly appetite this week and the scales said she'd lost two kilograms in the past month, which she couldn't quite believe.

Totally Laird's fault. When she thought about him, her appetite faded.

'You look good,' he said, and rested a hand against her shoulder blades for a lingering moment as he ushered her ahead of him towards the house. She hoped Sarah wasn't looking, and instinctively turned her head to check. She didn't want perceptive eight-year-old-girl questions...

No, it was fine. The girls had seen something in a nearby paddock—one that wasn't planted with vines and was at a diagonal to the house and just behind it. Three somethings, Tammy discovered as she looked more closely. A donkey and two ponies.

'Laird, you didn't tell me you had animals!'

'The kids aren't allergic, are they, or scared? They weren't at the zoo…'

'No, the opposite. They'll be in heaven.'

'The ponies are Amira and Banana, and the donkey is Solly. He's purely for decoration. I'm getting completely out of control with this hobby-farm thing, as you can tell.'

'Oh, I can! First a house, then vineyards and orchards and ponies. What's next, Laird?'

'I have a horrible feeling it'll be ducks and hand-reared lambs, and that I'll be pressing grapes into wine with my own bare feet.'

'You'll have to retire from medicine to take care of it all.'

'My neighbour agists several of her horses on my land for free, and takes care of these three in return.'

'Better get her permission on the hand-reared lambs, then.'

They grinned at each other.

'We can saddle the ponies and give the girls a ride, if they'd like,' Laird offered. 'My neighbour's kids ride them, and I'm told they're very good-tempered and safe. As well as nice and close to the ground.'

All three girls shrieked with excitement when they heard what was happening, and almost the whole morning was taken up with grooming and saddling, a sedate ride each for Laura and Lucy and a longer ride for Sarah in which Laird taught her some basic skills and positioning with stirrups and reins. She was in a transition phase at the moment, coming out of a little girl's dolls and fairies and into… Tammy didn't know quite what, and Sarah didn't seem to either. Ballet, maybe? Tennis?

Now the issue was settled.

After an hour in a paddock, Sarah was totally, utterly and permanently in love with ponies.

'Can I go faster?' she asked, just as Tammy was about to tell her she'd done enough for today. 'Can I trot?'

'Would you let her trot?' Laird asked. They looked at each other.

'I'm making a commitment here, aren't I?' Tammy realised out loud. 'If I let her go any further with this now, then one day I'm going to have to try and scrape up enough money for riding lessons. I'm going to have to watch her galloping over big wooden jumps with my heart in my mouth.'

'Those are the implications,' he agreed. 'Brave enough for it?'

Sarah was waiting for her answer. She'd brought the pony to a halt quite competently and was sitting on it with her face and shoulders screwed up tight, as if her whole destiny hinged on this moment. Despite the application of sunscreen, a scattering of freckles was already darkening on her face in the spring sunshine. She was a skinny, good-natured, energetic tomboy, and she'd been in heaven on the shaggy pony.

'Horses are risky,' Tammy murmured.

'Should I talk you out of it? Life is risky. Babies get born early for no reason. Space rocks fall out of the sky.'

'And people choke on apples, even though they're good for you. I know. That's what I've always believed. Embrace life, despite the risks.'

They were still looking at each other with wry smiles and complete understanding and that zing getting louder in the air. Was Laird only asking her about the risk of ponies? What other risks was he daring her to take?

For the moment, she only had an answer on this one.

Tammy raised her voice. 'You can trot, sweetheart, but listen to Laird when he tells you what to do.'

Laird strode across the grass and gave Sarah some instructions on telling a pony to go faster, corrected her heel position in the stirrups, showed her how to squeeze back the reins. 'He has a soft mouth, this lad, he doesn't need you to pull hard and hurt him.'

Sarah listened and nodded, then pulled on one rein and turned the pony towards the centre of the paddock. She kicked. Banana felt he'd had enough of carrying little girls today and didn't move.

'Harder, Sarah, you won't hurt him. He's being a bit lazy, wants to test out who's boss. You have to show him it's you.'

Sarah nodded and kicked again. Banana ambled off at a lazy walk.

'Even harder, sweetheart.'

This time, she took the word 'harder' a little too much to heart. Without warning, Banana broke into a bouncy, spirited canter and raced off through the grass. Sarah screamed…and so did her mother. Was that a sound of terror or pleasure, fading in the air as Banana carried Sarah wildly away?

'Oh, hell…' Laird muttered. 'This wasn't supposed to happen.'

He broke into a sprint and Tammy followed.

Seconds later, Sarah lost her seat, lost her stirrups and fell, while Banana cantered away and then slowed and wheeled around with a sheepish sort of air, as if he was a bit embarrassed at having gone off like that. He dropped his head and started munching on the grass.

'Is she…? Is she…?' Tammy gasped as she ran.

Was Sarah moving? She was. Her shoulders were shaking. She was sobbing. Or…

She sat up, laughing out loud. 'That was so-o-o fun!'

'Are you hurt, Sarah?' Tammy dropped to the grass beside her.

Sarah matter-of-factly examined a long grass stain on her forearm that would probably turn into a bruise, and rubbed at a couple of other places on her body. 'I'm a bit bumped,' she said.

'Were you scared, sweetheart?'

'Only right when I fell off. I loved going fast.'

'Let me take a little look at you, Sarah,' Laird said.

He did a quick neuro check then got her to turn her head, lift her arms, walk in a straight line. Tammy watched the interaction between them. Laird's straightforward calm, Sarah's quick obedience.

They were good together…and Sarah really was unhurt.

'Can I get back on?' she asked eagerly.

'Just to ride him over to the fence so we don't have so far to carry the tack,' Laird said.

He helped her back on. Banana gave Laird's stomach a nuzzle, as if in apology. Sarah got her feet back in the stirrups and the reins in the correct position in her hands, squared her shoulders and nudged the pony into a walk as if the fall had never happened.

People could choke on apples, but most of the time they were delicious and crunchy and good for you.

All three girls were adorable as they unsaddled Amira and Banana, after the alarming end to their ride, and gave the ponies and donkey some treats. They trailed after Laird, taking every one of his instructions seriously, staying away from the animals' back legs, willing to help with whatever he asked.

Laura and Lucy stretched up to hang the ponies' bridles on their hooks in the little tack room at one end of an impressive shed, while Sarah insisted on lugging one of the saddles all the way from the paddock fence, even though it weighed almost as much as she did.

By the time the ponies had been groomed and released again to roam their paddock freely, it was lunchtime. Laird had bought an assortment of pies from a local bakery earlier that morning. He put them into the oven to reheat and asked, 'Inside or out to eat?'

'Out,' Tammy answered, so they set up a table on the veranda, and the girls chomped down their chicken and vegetable pies in about five minutes then went back to talk to Amira, Banana and Solly over the fence, while Tammy and Laird lazed over their meal and drank two cups of tea.

They took a walk around the property, with the girls running ahead like puppies, jumping off stumps, balancing on logs, picking dandelions, chasing each other and falling into a laughing heap in the long spring grass.

'It still needs a lot doing to it,' Laird said as they headed back to the house.

'Oh, yes, you'll have to go to the garden centre nearly every week—what an unspeakable burden for you,' Tammy answered, enthusiastic and envious on his behalf.

He looked at her. 'Come to the garden centre with me. Help me choose.'

She didn't answer, because if he hadn't been serious, or if he changed his mind, the eager agreement that she could so easily have made would hang like a yoke around both their necks. She didn't dare to think beyond today. 'I'd better not. I'd make you spend too much,' she told him lightly.

Back at the house, the younger girls were ready for the box of dolls Tammy had put in the back of the van and Sarah still enjoyed the excuse to play at four-year-old level, while Laird wanted Tammy's advice in the kitchen on what to feed everyone that night. 'You're staying, right?'

'Well, we should probably—'

'You're staying.' He leaned closer. She could feel his body warmth, smell his shampoo, and feel her own surging reaction to him.

OK, he was right, they were staying.

For dinner, they decided on a green salad and cheese ravioli, with a sauce they just made up out of things they found in the pantry. Canned tomatoes and chopped capers, a shake of dried herbs, a handful of crushed walnuts, parmesan cheese to go on top.

'I wish we lived here,' Sarah announced after the meal, and Tammy had to hide her head in the fridge while she put away the leftover salad, so that her face didn't say far too clearly to Laird that she did, too.

'You can't stay the whole night, can you?' Laird asked quietly, while the girls were packing up their dolls. 'I shouldn't even ask.'

'Mel's dropping the boys off at eight-thirty in the morning. Mum would be worried.'

'Even if you phoned her?'

'Especially if I phoned her. Laura and Lucy are tired. I really have to go. They've had a terrific day.'

'So have I,' said Laird quietly.

* * *

But the minivan wouldn't start.

Laird had found the chance to kiss Tammy in the kitchen at last, ten minutes earlier, and she'd had to tear herself away from the warmth of his arms. Now she had the girls all bundled in the car, yawning, and the box of dolls packed in the back. It was dark. The ponies and the donkey were quiet beneath their shelter in the paddock...

And the wretched van just wouldn't start.

Which was appropriate somehow. An omen, probably.

A perfect day, coming to a wobbly, uncomfortable, typical-for-Tammy end.

Tammy had to phone Mum to tell her not to worry because they weren't home yet, phone Mel to say good-night to the boys, and finally phone the road service, who took forty minutes to arrive, couldn't get the van started either and came up with a direly expensive-sounding list of things that needed to be done to it before it could be driven again.

They towed it away to the garage Laird recommended, by which time the girls' yawns had turned into fretfulness and complaints. It was way past their bedtime.

'I'll drive you,' Laird said.

When they pulled up in her driveway after eleven o'clock, Laura, Lucy and Sarah were all asleep in his back seat, and Mum had to be asleep out the back because there were no lights on. Tammy had told her not to wait up for them. Laird carried Sarah inside, while Tammy carried Laura, then she changed the half-asleep girls into their nightwear while Laird went back to the car for Lucy.

It was eleven-thirty by the time they were settled.

Tammy came back downstairs and straight into Laird's

waiting arms, not because she'd planned to but because he was standing there waiting for her in the living-room and he held them out and she couldn't...didn't want to...do anything else. 'Come here, you...'

'Thank you for today.'

'Stop. No talking.'

He kissed her, tenderly at first, as if to soothe away the bumps in their evening, then harder and deeper because the need had built up inside him all day. Tammy could feel the release of it now all through his strong body—an eagerness and urgency and celebration of the fact that he had her alone at last.

She couldn't believe that he wanted her so much, couldn't understand why, couldn't trust it, but felt herself swept away with it anyhow, because she didn't have enough strength to say no. There was just a chance she could fight him, but she couldn't fight herself at the same time.

'Here or upstairs?' he said. 'Tammy, I want this so much.' He ran his hands over her breasts beneath their thin covering of outer cotton and inner lace, and over the tops of her thighs, and that too-curvy and generous jeans-clad rear end that was supposed to protect her from something like this.

'It's brutal, how much I want this,' he muttered. He pulled at her cotton top and she helped him take it over her head and discard it on the floor.

'Is it?'

'Can't you feel it?' He bent to make a trail of kisses down her neck, toward the valley between her breasts.

*Yes. But can I trust it?*

Could she trust him or herself or the future or anything?

He slid the straps of her bra down her arms, pulled his

own shirt over his head, wrapped his arms hard around her again so that they stood skin to skin from the waist up, just two pairs of grass-stained jeans in the way of full intimacy. 'Stop me now, if you're going to, because…' He broke off and swore. 'I just want this.'

'I want it, too,' she whispered. She couldn't fight it any longer, couldn't remember all the reasons for saying no.

'Where?'

'Here?'

'Perfect.'

He ran his fingers around the back of her neck and up into her hair, painting kisses onto her skin in a dozen different places. Now that they both knew it was going to happen, there was no impatience or rush. He seemed to want to linger, to explore, to claim her whole body bit by bit, kiss by kiss.

She touched him, too, intensely aroused by the newness of him, by everything her senses began to learn about the way he felt and tasted. She'd lost track of the passing minutes by the time he brought his hands to the waistband of her jeans and whispered, 'Can we take these off? I want to hold you against me. I want to touch you…'

'Mmm.' Tammy unsnapped the fastening—not on her jeans but on his—and found him straining against the softer cotton of his dark-coloured briefs.

She felt a powerful, aching surge of anticipation at the thought of his size, of the way he would fill her, and was a little shocked at the greediness of her response. No denying it, though, she wanted him big and as close as a man could ever be. They both slid down their jeans and underwear and left them on the floor, forgotten.

'Oh,' he gasped as she touched him.

She felt him shudder as he wrapped his arms around her, and knew that they weren't going to be slow and unhurried about this for much longer, which meant...

'Do you have something?' she gabbled on a breathless, inpatient whisper. He felt like hot satin, and she felt a terrible, aching temptation to forget that kind of caution about birth control—but she couldn't. 'Protection, I mean...'

He took his hot mouth away from her neck. 'I do. Do we need it?'

'You've seen the size of my family, Laird. I'd have thought my fertility was well and truly proven.'

'So after the triplets, you didn't...? I mean, you could still have more children.'

'Yes, so...'

'Yes, OK. Wait.' He held her shoulders and lowered her to the couch, then kissed her until they almost forgot what had given them pause. Eventually he let her go and she watched him as he went in search of his wallet, loving the strength and ease and unselfconsciousness of his body in the bluish darkness, loving the instant heat of him as soon as he came back to her. 'You feel so good,' he whispered.

'So do you.'

'I've wanted this all day. Every time I looked at you.'

'Me, too.'

'To be inside you, to feel your legs wrapped around me and hear the sounds you make...'

After that, there was no more talking for a long time, and they fell asleep in each other's arms.

Tammy was the first to wake up. The clock on the DVD player read 2:15. Laird lay heavy and warm against her side and she could have stayed like this all night, cradling her own happiness the way she cradled his body. Her arm rested on his chest and her breasts nudged his ribs and chest with their fullness and weight. Her legs were tangled with his.

So she'd done it.

She'd given herself to a man—to him, to Laird—without promises or commitments or any certainty at all.

And she wasn't sorry. How could she be, when he was still here? There was an aura of trust in the way he slept, his chest rising and falling so peacefully, his lashes long and dark on his cheeks. She felt her own capacity for tenderness swelling inside her—the giving part of her, which just got so much *practice*, with the kids, with her work. She was good at giving. Too good. She liked it too much, and didn't protect herself enough.

She knew that, but she didn't want to change.

Yet she didn't want to get hurt either.

Laird stirred. She felt the difference in his breathing and knew he was awake, even though he hadn't opened his eyes. 'Mmm, Tammy...' he said.

'Hi, you.'

His heavy, sleepy lids lifted and he smiled a slow smile, and she couldn't help leaning across his body at once to kiss him. His hand brushed her backside as she moved, and her breasts grazed his chest and pressed into him. He touched her, brushing the ball of his thumb across her nipple, then he kissed her mouth and cupped her breasts in his hands so he could kiss them, too.

Again? Could she do this again? Was he going to stay all night and be here in the morning for the girls to find? She could imagine him dressing quickly the moment sounds started upstairs, refusing breakfast, leaving before they'd had any chance at a morning-after talk. He might make that vaguest of male promises, 'I'll call you,' and she wouldn't know where she stood.

The emotional vulnerability she'd recognised in herself so clearly just now had a physical counterpart in her naked body, entwined with his. The touch of his mouth on her nipples was so intimate and sweet. She gripped his shoulders and arched her back and had to fight within herself to push him away instead of pulling him closer.

'I think maybe...'

Maybe what? Maybe she wanted him to go home? Maybe she wanted him to promise undying love?

She slid sideways again, away from that so intimate press of their bodies and the touch of his mouth.

'What's up, Tammy?' he said softly.

'Just... Don't hurt me,' she heard herself say.

'What? Hell, Tammy, did I? Just now? You should have—'

'No...no. I don't mean hurt physically. Of course you didn't. You were— I meant my heart.' She pressed her closed hand between her breasts, and her back against the cushioned back of the couch.

'Tammy—'

'You told me to stop you, before, if I was going to stop you at all. And I didn't. But maybe I should have.'

'Is that what you're doing this time? Stopping me? Once is OK, but not twice?'

'I know it doesn't make sense. Why is *after* always so different from *before*?' She tried to laugh but it didn't quite work. 'I—I have to find out if I'm safe. My heart. My spirit. That's what I meant about hurting. I have to say this, Laird. If this has been a one-night stand...'

'It's not,' he said at once. 'It wasn't. How could it be, after we've—?'

'Then what is it?' She shivered as she spoke. This late at night, the room had grown chilly, especially when she wasn't letting herself take Laird's body warmth any more. She sat up, reached out to grab for her top, discarded two hours ago on the floor, and held it against her body. The protection it offered wasn't enough.

'Does it need a definition? Does it need a plan?' He pulled her close against him once more, and she could see his growing frustration.

A huge part of her wanted to let this go—this foolish, vulnerable protest of hers—and just kiss him again, ravish her mouth over every inch of him, even more intimately this time, feel his body against hers once more, give them both this whole night and think about the consequences in the morning, but she summoned some resolve and forced the issue.

'You can't date a divorced mother of five on a whim, Laird.' Her voice shook a little.

'This wasn't a whim. It isn't. How could you think that? Have I ever given that impression?'

'You haven't. But then what is it, Laird? A commitment? After we've been out together three times?'

'Four. I'm counting the garden centre.'

She laughed unwillingly. 'Don't.'

'Don't count the garden centre?'

'Don't make me laugh.'

He grew serious again. 'Is that what you're asking for? A commitment? So soon?'

'No. I'm asking for you to think about my children. And me. Think about me. You're always telling me I don't think enough about myself.'

'You don't.'

'So now I am, and I'm asking you to. Look at my baggage, and the reality of my life! Think about—oh, hell—the way I've been hurt before. By the man I once trusted with my whole life. Is there any way you'd ever be prepared to take on five of that man's kids? What would you get in return?'

'Do we have to—?'

'Don't tell me that question isn't important,' she cut in, a little shakily. 'Or that I'm asking it too soon, that we don't have to talk about it now. Now is exactly when it's important, and exactly when I have to ask. When there's still time to pull back, on both sides—just—without leaving my children hurt and confused. And me. Hurt wouldn't begin to cover it.'

'Are you confused?' He tried to kiss her again. 'Do you not know how you feel?'

'I—I think I might know too well how I feel, and I'm scared of it.'

'I did pretty well at the vineyard today, and afterwards.' He was smiling, not angry, teasing her, taking it all too lightly, still not seeing how much she meant this, how hard she was prepared to fight for her family, even if it meant fighting against herself and her own heart.

'You did brilliantly,' she agreed. 'For one day.'

'That counts for nothing?' His tone was still patient,

gentle, still a little teasing. 'The girls seem to like me, Tammy, and the boys did, too, last week. Hell, we kidded each other about the zoo being a big exam, but it really was one, wasn't it? And so was today. I scored well on the ponies, I guess...'

'Yes, you did, but—'

'What else do I have to do? How many hoops are there that I have to jump through here?' Now, finally, he sounded as if he was getting impatient and prepared to be angry if necessary, the way ambitious doctors often did when they struck incompetence or slow thinking.

Tammy held her ground. 'I'm not being unreasonable. You're an intelligent man, Laird. You can flatten me with an argument, throw out your professional superiority if you want, but that doesn't mean I'm wrong and you're right.'

'So make me understand,' he invited her quietly.

'You do understand. You will if you think about it. Stop letting our bodies get in the way.' Hers still was. Far too much. 'My children are going to be around for the rest of my life.'

'I do know that.'

'They're not a trivial impediment. They're asleep under this roof right now. They—they *matter*. They're expensive. They're tiring. And they're not teenagers yet! They're in my life and in my heart twenty-four hours of every day. They make me vulnerable, and I would have been vulnerable even without them, after Tom left.'

'And you need to know if they could be in my heart the same way.'

'You need to think about it. Really and seriously think about it, in a way you've probably never had to think about a relationship before. Don't...don't sweep me off my feet and…and make love to me again, and expect it all to fall into place in the morning. It won't. Sex…more sex…doesn't answer the questions I need answered.'

'This isn't just sex, Tammy.'

She ignored him. 'Even worse, don't plan to renege on it in the morning. I don't want to sleep with a man whenever he asks, give myself to a man over and over in that vital, intimate way—maybe sex isn't like that for you, but it is for me, I won't pretend about it—and then have him say in a few days or a few weeks, *Oops, yeah, the kids are a bit much, now that you mention it. And our different circumstances, too. Should have realised before. Think I'll back off.* Please, take some more time to think. Please, let's both cool off for a while before we go any further with this and see if anything changes.'

'That's really what you want?' He kissed her, brushing her mouth with his lips. 'For us to cool off? You think that's the only way to work this out?'

'It's the only way for me. I'm sorry. But it is. I—I probably should have… My body got in the way tonight.'

'Your body is beautiful.'

'Don't.'

There was a beat of silence. 'OK, then, if that's what you're really asking for, that's what I'll do.' He hugged and held her one last time, his arms strong but yielding, as if her body were some fragile thing that might break beneath his touch. How long since anyone had treated her as fragile? 'I want to give you whatever you need, Tammy, that's the bottom line.'

'Do it now,' she whispered, struggling. 'Go now. Don't let me change my mind.'

'Might you?'

'I might. So easily. And then I'd be angry with you.'

'I wouldn't want that,' he said lightly.

They looked at each other for a long, frozen moment that might have lasted thirty seconds or a hundred and thirty, Tammy had no idea. Laird's grey eyes were clouded. When he broke their eye contact, it was to look around the room, with that how-did-I-get-here expression on his face that she'd seen before.

'You're right,' he finally said. 'We do need to do this. There's too much at stake to let our impulses and our instincts rule.'

'They're notoriously unreliable, aren't they?' she said, as light as he'd been through most of this.

But her voice shook and they both flinched at the level of emotion in the air. Only a minute or two later she stood in the middle of the room listening to the fading sound of his car down the street.

# CHAPTER NINE

'YOU'VE done the right thing,' Tarsha decreed, over dinner at a little Italian place near her townhouse on Sunday night. 'Absolutely the right thing.'

'You haven't heard the full story yet,' Laird said, feeling an absurd need to confess every detail of his sleeplessness, his dizzy thoughts, the way his heart lifted when he thought about Tammy's hair and her laugh and how she looked when she was bending over her children.

Tarsha quirked her mouth and drawled, 'Do I need to? You've said you're not seeing her any more.'

'No, I've said we're not seeing each other for the moment. We're cooling off and taking time to think. That's different.'

He'd been clinging to the difference all last night and through today, while at the same time feeling appalled at the strength of his own feelings. He'd come so close to turning his car around in the street last night and hammering on her front door.

*Let me in. I'll love you forever. Marry me.*

But he wasn't that kind of a man. He was rational, capable. When he had a big decision to make, he thought it through from all angles. How long had he thought about which medical specialty would best fit his skills? How many Yarra Valley properties had he looked at before settling on the vineyard? How many car dealers did he torment every time he bought a new car? He wouldn't know how to mess up his life with a rash decision if he tried. Yet here he was—

'How is it different?' Tarsha demanded. 'Why?'

'She's asked me to take some time to think. Which I really respect.'

'Time to think? Laird, that's exactly the easy out that both of you need. The whole thing will go away in a few weeks.'

'I'm not looking for an easy out, I'm not looking for Tammy to go away, I'm looking for...' Laird ground to a halt.

'You see? You don't know, do you?'

*Yes, I do.*

But that was too irrational a possibility to contemplate.

'Certainty,' he said out loud.

'Any strategies for finding it? Share them with me, would you?' Tarsha jibed.

'Cynicism is very aging, Tarsh. Be careful.'

She slumped suddenly. 'Well, I am cynical about love. And certainty. I was certain a few months ago. He wasn't. End of story. No happily ever after.'

'What's his name?'

'Olivier. You had to make me say it, didn't you?'

'And you can't get him out of your system.'

'No. And I'm not sure how I ever will.'

No. Exactly.

Laird felt as if Tammy was growing around his heart and his life like a flower-laden vine, entwined with him, necessary to him, making him better in half a dozen different ways than he could ever be on his own. So different. So new. So unexpected. And so right.

'Infatuations can manifest that way,' Tarsha said, as if she'd read his thoughts and was commenting on them. 'Bad things happen. Love is one-sided, temporary, delusional. I'm cynical, Laird, but that doesn't mean I'm wrong!'

'I—I— Yes, I know.' He sighed.

It was true. Sensible men fell hard for the worst women and destroyed their own lives. Well-grounded women got stars in their eyes and couldn't see when a man was total bad news. Two people thought they'd found the pot of gold at the end of the rainbow, and then the light changed and it turned to dust. Those things happened. How did you tell if it was happening to you? What part of yourself did you trust? What wisdom from friends did you listen to?

But Tarsha had delivered her advice and was ready to talk about something else. 'Cup Day on Tuesday, Laird,' she said, businesslike. 'We're still on for that?'

'Yes, if you want to.' He attempted to drag his own thoughts onto a more sensible level. He had to function. He couldn't fall into a gibbering heap over Tammy Prunty. Somehow, being able to function as a normal, rational human being seemed like a piece of necessary proof that what he felt for her was real.

'I do want to,' Tarsha said. 'I need you.'

'Handbag duty again?'

'Exactly!'

They'd arranged it weeks ago. She had hard-to-come-by invitations for a corporate marquee hosted by a major cosmetics corporation, L'Occidentale, and knew two or three of the racehorse owners. She planned on schmoozing with the right people, and had her eye on several women and a couple of men who were entering the Fashions on the Field contest, with the view to taking them on as models when her new agency launched in a few weeks' time. The Melbourne Cup was Australia's biggest race of the year, and the carnival was a huge event for fashion buffs, too.

Laird had jockeyed for a day off this coming Tuesday the way the top riders would jockey for position during the race itself, because nobody wanted to work on Cup Day. Since he'd covered long hours for other doctors last Melbourne Cup Day, as well as at Christmas, New Year and Easter, he was owed this one.

'I'll pick you up,' he told her manfully, and named a time, which she promptly countered with her own suggestion of an hour earlier.

'Really?'

'In case I need to fix you up.'

'Fix me up?'

'Your hair. Your suit. Your shoes.' She tilted her head and gave a beguiling smile, but then her eyes filled with sudden tears. 'Laird, I really need Tuesday to be a good day.'

Several people in the NICU at Yarra Hospital needed Tuesday to be a good day, and Tammy knew it had nothing to do with which horse they were planning to bet on in the Cup. With big plans of her own for race day this year, she fully intended to have a flutter on the Cup herself, but she had to get through the rest of Monday first.

Day Two of the rest of her life.

Life after Laird.

Life beyond the brief rainbow-butterfly-magical feeling of Laird.

He'd gone away to think, and she was pretty sure what his thoughts would eventually tell him—exactly the same thing as they were telling her. It couldn't last. It couldn't work. He didn't need a woman like her, he needed someone thin and single and gorgeous who would finish off his successful life with an attractive flourish, the way a decorative bow finished a gift-wrapped package.

Tammy had spent two hours before her shift this morning driving out to the Yarra Valley garage near Laird's place to pick up the van. She wasn't convinced it was going to be drivable much longer, even if she spent hundreds of dollars more on getting bits of it fixed. This was her reality, not that wonderful day she'd spent with Laird and the girls at the vineyard on Saturday, and with Laird at her own house late into the night.

Reality was the hospital and the babies she cared about.

Harry Vitelli had his eyes tested that afternoon. Thirty minutes before the procedure, Tammy had to put in the eye drops he needed for local anaesthesia and to dilate his pupils.

'Here we go, sweetheart,' she murmured, then watched her own hand tremble and miss, so that the first drop ran down the baby's cheek. Biting her lips and willing her fingers to stay steady this time, she got the drops where they belonged, thankful that Alison hadn't been looking on.

The ophthalmologist was coming to the baby, rather than the baby being taken elsewhere. Whenever possible, it worked this way in the NICU. Procedures and even surgery on premature babies was done in the unit to minimise the handling and disturbance of the baby, as well as making it easier to maintain ongoing treatment.

'You've put the drops in?' Alison asked, when she came back from the bathroom. Her mother was at home with baby Brittany, who should be weaned off her oxygen this week. 'What happens if the doctor is late?'

'He won't be. He knows where we're up to.'

'Will we know right away if it's at stage three?'

Stage three retinopathy was the threshold for using laser treatment. The ophthalmologist would look at several key criteria, including the severity and location of the disorder and other clinical abnormalities in the cornea, lens or iris. But this was only the first of Harry's eye tests, which meant that a good result at this point didn't necessarily mean Alison or her husband could relax.

'Yes, he'll talk to you about all that once he's taken a good look,' Tammy told her. 'How about you go and grab a coffee and something to eat, Alison? Get back a bit later, when Dr Tran is finishing up.'

Alison nodded and pressed her lips together. 'Maybe that's best.'

Laird walked past at that moment, and his eyes met Tammy's—one brief flash of contact that she couldn't interpret. She often caught him looking at her when she was talking to parents and it threw her off balance every time. She pushed him out of her mind while she assisted Dr Tran. Alison came back just as he was putting his equipment away.

He'd found extensive stage two ROP in the baby's left eye, but no problems so far in his right. Alison and her husband had been given information to read about retinopathy of prematurity, and Tammy told her after Dr Tran had given a clear and careful report, 'If you have any questions now, or think of any later, please ask. Write them down as they come to you, so you don't forget. This isn't something we want you to have any uncertainties about.'

'We can deal with it,' Alison said. 'It's OK. If it gets to threshold level, they'll treat it. That's right, isn't it?'

'That's it, yes.'

'Hopefully it won't progress. And I liked the doctor. I saw the way he touched Harry. Gentle. I appreciate that so much. When he's had so many hands on him, so many things that make him flinch and make his oxygen go down.'

But, still, the presence of stage two retinopathy wasn't the good news Alison had hoped for. Tammy gave her a hug and told her gently, 'Hang in, there,' while wishing there were much better words.

Meanwhile little Max Parry was still in the HDU and had taken no backward steps. His weight had climbed to over 1100 grams. Adam, however, weighed only just over 700 grams. They'd been trialling him for several days on full milk feeds and giving him regular and increasing breaks from CPAP to see how well he breathed on his own.

Adam hadn't shown any problems on CPAP at first and had seemed to be getting stronger and healthier in other ways, too, 'And I was stupid,' sobbed Fran to Tammy on Monday evening. 'I said to Chris that it looked like he'd turned the corner, and then this happens.'

'This' was a serious apnoea episode earlier that afternoon, followed by three significant vomits. Now his gut had swollen and Fran knew enough about premature babies by now to understand the risks. Adam was put on increased antibiotics, put back on the ventilator after the scary episode of forgetting to breathe, and put back on intravenous nutrition instead of milk feeds.

Backward steps, all of them.

Tammy felt as if she understood too much about those. She'd been taking backward steps since Laird had left her house on Saturday night. Back to the doubt that any man could find her attractive with the amount of baggage she carried—precious baggage, true, but her baggage, not his.

She knew she'd done the right thing, asking him to take some time, to really think about what he wanted and what he could give. But, oh, it didn't feel like the right thing!

She was such a fool! All she wanted was to find him at her front door with…what…a bottle of champagne, an armful of flowers, a pair of board shorts and a beach towel, a pile of his shirts to iron, for heaven's sake! Anything, as long as it came with huge, wonderful promises and lifelong declarations and a great big passionate sweep off her feet and into his arms.

*I don't need time to think, Tammy, sweetheart, I just need you.*

It didn't happen.

No phone call, no appearance, no flowers or board shorts or crumpled shirts or sweeping, just silence and the painful prospect of seeing him regularly at work for the next thousand or so years, while all the hurt and vulnerability that Tom had delivered into Tammy's life became magnified a hundred times because of Laird.

Meanwhile, if Adam developed necrotising enterocolitis at his current size, he wouldn't survive. Surgery on such a small baby's bowel would be so risky and delicate, it verged on the impossible. At nine-thirty on Monday night,

Laird and surgeon Ralph Goode were still assessing the tiny boy, trying to work out what was going on and what, if anything, they could do.

'The X-ray wasn't clear enough,' Laird said to Dr Goode, in the night-time quiet of the unit. 'Tammy, can you please put it up so we can take another look?'

She nodded, found the X-ray envelope, slid the pictures out and clipped them against the light-box on a nearby wall. She was painfully aware of Laird while she did it, and she could so easily read the studied way he avoided her eye, then helplessly caught it once or twice, making the air zing. If either the Parrys or Dr Goode noticed any kind of tension, she couldn't tell.

What was he thinking? She wanted to touch him, throw herself onto him and tell him, *I didn't mean it. Don't think. Just take me to bed again. Just look at me again the way you did this afternoon when I was talking to Alison. Tell me with those eyes of yours that you want me and I'm yours.*

The two doctors looked at the X-rays together, Laird tracing his lean fingers over the confusing shadings of black and grey and white as he talked. 'It could be a blockage, but I'm not prepared to make that diagnosis on the basis of a picture like this. He had a blood transfusion late this afternoon. His blood gases have improved...' He trailed off.

The word 'but' hung unspoken in the air. Fran wiped her eyes with the tissues Chris passed her. He had an expression of powerless anger and pain on his face, while they both clung to every word the doctors said.

'And there's no sign of active infection?' Dr Goode asked.

'No, the antibiotics are a preventative, rather than a response.'

Dr Goode palpated the baby's fragile, distended abdomen with gloved hands and an incredibly sure, delicate touch, then applied a warmed stethoscope and listened. He was in his early fifties, and gave off a calm authority and air of experience that the Parrys must feel and find reassuring. 'I'm hearing some bowel sounds. If it's a blockage, it's not complete. Rest his gut, and let's wait and see. It may resolve on its own.'

'Mr and Mrs Parry, are you happy with that plan?' Laird asked.

'Is there another option?' Chris asked.

'Not really. Surgery would be a last-ditch measure.'

'The reality is he'd be unlikely to survive it, let alone be helped by it,' said Dr Goode. 'There's no point softening what we tell you on this.'

Fran nodded, her throat working.

'Let's go and see Max,' Chris said gently to his wife.

But Fran shook her head and pushed him away. 'I want to stay here.' Her fists were clenched as if pure willpower would keep her baby alive.

'Beautiful, Max needs us just as much. Don't give him less because he's healthier. Come with me and let's just sit with him for a while.'

'OK. All right.' She nodded tiredly and he led her out of the unit, and Laird and Dr Goode departed, too, leaving Tammy alone with little Adam.

Twenty minutes later, he pooed.

'And we're thrilled about it, baby,' Tammy cooed softly to him as she changed his tiny envelope of a nappy. 'You wait until I tell your mummy!'

And Laird.

It was scary how much she looked forward to telling Laird, and how disappointed she was when she discovered he'd gone home without seeking her out, even to say goodnight.

*He's thinking. He's giving us both some distance. It's what you asked for, so trust it.*

But trust, after a betrayal, was so scary and hard.

'How about we make a deal, you and me?' she told a briefly wakeful baby Adam, after Fran and Chris had gone home at around ten-thirty. They seemed to be feeling more cheerful after Adam's encouraging bowel movement, and the NICU had gone quiet and dark for the night, with only one or two parents still slumped tiredly in uncomfortable chairs, and the frieze of 'graduate' babies just a blur on the wall.

'No more backward steps, OK?' Tammy said softly to the baby. 'We'll keep each other on track. You grow and get strong and remember to breathe right…and so will I. Is it a deal? I have too much to do in my life, too much else to think about, to let Laird Burchell mean so much, to spend so much of my time and effort fighting to trust him.'

## CHAPTER TEN

'I CANNOT get this hat to work!' Tarsha said viciously, blinking back tears.

'So try a different one,' Laird suggested in a soothing voice.

Wrong answer.

So far today, Tarsha didn't seem too impressed at how he was performing in his role of suave professional handbag. He couldn't blame her. His heart wasn't in it. His heart was with a copper-haired, sumptuous-bodied nurse who made his whole soul burn with questions that he couldn't yet answer and didn't know how he ever would.

'Do you *honestly* think I have another hat just lying around that will match this outfit?' Tarsha gestured at her slip of a dress in beige silk and lace, her tiny jacket and her barely there spike-heeled shoes. 'And if you suggest trying a different outfit…!'

'I think the hat looks great.' His thoughts were miles away.

'You're not taking this seriously.'

Making the effort to focus, Laird told her, 'Well, I did think the Melbourne Cup was more about horses than clothes.'

He almost had the impression that Tarsha wasn't taking

it seriously either, despite her anger. It seemed as if she was using the hat and his own thick-headedness about fashion as a way to vent other sources of stress. If that was the case, he knew better than to ask for a direct explanation. She'd get to the point if and when she was ready.

'Are you *kidding*?' she exclaimed. 'I was so lucky to get the invites from L'Occidentale.' Her whole demeanour suddenly changed. She pressed her lips together and took a deep breath. One beautifully manicured hand rested for a moment above her left breast. 'But you're right. It's not important, is it? Not in the scheme of things. I don't know what I'm doing today...' She cast him a narrow, sideways glance and opened her mouth as if to speak again, then shook her head and sighed. 'Let's just go to the races,' she muttered.

'Take your time, Tarsha,' he soothed her again, at a loss to know what he was dealing with here. 'Check your make-up. I'll wait.' She seemed as highly strung as one of the thoroughbreds they were going to watch.

'No. You're right. I'll leave the hat. It truly is not important,' she said again, as if she really meant it.

As far as Tammy was concerned, there was absolutely no point in taking the Melbourne Cup fashion thing seriously.

She wouldn't have gone to the event at all, under normal circumstances, but several friends had followed through on the threat they'd made this time last year, after she'd organised a Mini Melbourne Cup Party in the back garden for her own children and eight of their little mates, complete with hobby-horse races and dress-ups and colourful food. In Victoria, the Tuesday of 'The Race That Stops A Nation' was a public holiday, and there was no school.

'Next year, Tammy, two of us are babysitting, and the other two are taking you to the races,' Liz had said after the kids' Cup party.

'Which two of you are doing which?'

'Whoever wins first and second in our Cup sweep today gets to stay home with the kids,' Kelly declared.

So at nine-thirty in the morning a year later—i.e. today—Mel had swooped in and carried all five kids off to her place, where Bron was already setting up some games, and Kelly and Liz had marched Tammy into her bedroom to help her with her wardrobe.

'I already have the hat,' she told them helpfully, then watched them shriek in delight—or was it horror?—at the large, floppy-brimmed wheel of cream straw festooned with green organza ribbon, fake leaves and a ring of bright red plastic chillies. She and Sarah had had a lot of fun and hilarity putting it together on Sunday afternoon. For almost a whole half an hour, her heart hadn't ached about Laird.

This morning, she was determined not to let her friends know how churned up she was feeling. They didn't yet know that Laird existed, and she didn't intend to tell them. Sarah might let something slip, she realised. Hopefully Mel and Bron would keep the kids too busy for an eight-year-old to think about it.

'All right,' Liz said calmly. 'You really *aren't* taking the fashion thing seriously. Now, what can we put with it?'

'Well, my wardrobe is simply crammed with designer outfits, as you can imagine.' Tammy laughed. 'Take a look.'

Liz ended up driving back to her place to bring an armload of possibilities, and they settled on an elegantly floaty panelled skirt and a shoulder-baring silk camisole, neither of which was the same colour green as any of the three different greens on the hat, but, as Kelly said, it didn't matter.

'It's more a symphony of greens,' she decreed. 'It works. Really shows off your figure.'

'You mean it makes me look fat?'

'Womanly, Tammy. The word is womanly.'

She decreed that the spare plastic chillies pinned artistically around the slightly-lower-than-Tammy-was-happy-with neckline of the camisole worked, too.

'And the sash,' Liz insisted. 'The red silk sash.' She tied it in place, puffing out the loop of the bow.

Tammy groaned. 'Oh, I'm going to be so loud!'

'Much more interesting than our drippy pastels.'

'No, you both look lovely.'

'So do you.'

'In a loud kind of way. Like a big red apple hanging on a tree.'

And yet she felt like dressing loud today.

When in doubt, shout.

Or something.

Through the sheer audacity of wearing to the Melbourne Cup a whole orchestral, apple-hued arrangement of red and green with her copper-and-carrots hair and finishing the outfit off with scarlet shoes, Tammy could shut out the sound of that nagging, aching, vulnerable little voice inside her every time she thought about Laird, about trusting him—whether she dared to, whether there was any chance he'd come up with an answer to their future that wouldn't hurt.

The outfit almost worked, too, until an hour after arriving, when, temporarily parted from her two friends, she saw Laird himself and the whole day suddenly changed, like a fierce storm sweeping in to cut down baking summer heat.

He stood just beyond the mounting yard, inspecting the horses before the fourth race. He was wearing a suit, so well cut it could have been Armani, with a flower in his lapel, and there was a gorgeously clad, elegantly thin, model-beautiful woman in a vintage couture dress and six-inch heels leaning intimately on his arm and smiling.

And Tammy felt ill.

Physically ill. Sick to her stomach, head dizzy and pounding, skin breaking out in a cold sweat, limbs gone weak. Oh, she remembered this! It was exactly the way she'd felt the day she'd come home to find Tom packing his things in their bedroom, when he hadn't even told her yet that he planned to leave.

She stood there and watched Laird, appalled by the power and suddenness of her reaction. She couldn't move. Her throat was choked. It felt like solid ground collapsing without warning beneath her feet, and it was horrible. Familiar and horrible. She couldn't have spoken a word, even if Kelly and Liz had been standing right beside her, demanding to know what was wrong. The sounds of the crowd faded, and for a moment Tammy was afraid she might actually faint.

The woman smiled again. Laird nodded. The woman nudged his shoulder and pointed at something. They were together. That was all Tammy knew. Here she was in the flesh, the mythical woman Tammy had talked about to Laird when they'd argued over him sending cleaners in after the kids had been sick.

Thin, single and gorgeous.

She wasn't an abstract possibility—the woman he *should* be going out with, the theoretical opposite to Tammy herself, the woman he *would* go out with one day, when Tammy herself was long forgotten—she was already real.

There was no room for anything inside her but the sheer, physical hurt of it. Betrayal like a knife thrust. Disbelief like an onslaught of white noise. Shock thundering through her bloodstream like the hooves on the track.

*What a fool I am...*

Trust? Where did trust fit in now?

She honestly hadn't considered that she might have a rival so soon or, worse, that she might have had one all along. How long had these two known each other? For a while, judging by the way they were talking. There was something so casual and familiar about the woman's hold on Laird's arm, about the way he nodded at something she said without turning to look at her.

Tammy thought she had fully considered the harsh reality that Laird didn't belong in her life. She'd told herself more than once that he should be going out with that gorgeous, thin, designer-dressed model she'd conjured up for him.

But, oh, she hadn't really meant it!

*And he is going out with her*, said the evidence of her eyes, until her vision was blinded by tears, at which point all she could do was to stand there, blinking, waiting for her heart to recover the correct beat.

'You'll have to hurry if you're going to put on a bet, Laird,' Tarsha pointed out.

'I won't put one on this race,' Laird said. 'No clue about any of these horses.'

They all looked magnificent. Their rich chestnut and chocolate coats gleamed in the sun, their bodies moved with incomparable power and grace and you could see how highly strung they were, positively eager to prove their worth at top speed.

But how did you tell about their heart and soul? It was the question that consumed him. Whether you were considering horses or your own heart, how did you tell what mattered, what ran bone deep, what was lasting and important and real?

'Most other people don't have a clue about the horses today, and it's not stopping them,' Tarsha said with a smile.

'True.' Laird was briefly distracted by the flare of her sharp humour, which hadn't been much in evidence so far today. He flicked his gaze briefly in her direction and grinned at her. She was a good person, a far cry from the stereotype of the bitchy model.

He wasn't by any means a gambler, but it was a national tradition to put money on horses on Cup Day, as Tarsha had implied, and almost an act of treason not to. The whole of Flemington Racecourse was crowded with once-a-year punters.

'So can we put on a bet and then go back to the marquee?' she asked, cajoling him.

'It's your feet in those shoes,' he guessed. 'You want to sit down. My arm's not doing enough, even though you're practically dragging it from its socket.'

'And I'll attempt to schmooze some more and have another great big glass of champagne...'

She'd already had one, although it wasn't yet much past noon. Laird was a little surprised. Tarsha drank roughly the same amount as he gambled—in other words, not much. She seemed to be putting on a performance today. Her smiles didn't reach her eyes, beneath that shadowy confection of a hat, and a distant look appeared on her face whenever she wasn't talking. What was going on? Whatever it was, he shouldn't ignore what she wanted.

'All right, we'll go back,' he said, turning with Tarsha's arm still linked through his.

And that was when he saw Tammy.

Like an apparition manifesting in a magical way from a slightly obsessive corner of his thoughts, she was suddenly there, right in front of him, standing on the worn-out grass as if she'd forgotten how to move. She looked terrific, in a very Tammy way. Bright and fun and lavishly shaped, and not in any danger of taking herself too seriously. Not with those chillies on her hat.

She'd clearly seen him several minutes earlier but had been pretending very hard that she hadn't. More chillies garlanded the ruffled neckline of her silk top, and he had to fight not to give a lingering, appreciative look down at her fabulous sumptuous figure, all curvy and generous and fine-skinned and a little more on show than usual.

And he was so instinctively, unthinkingly happy to see her—the sun seemed brighter, the race day atmosphere instantly more interesting and meaningful—that he didn't understand what her problem was until it was far too late.

'You're here, too,' he began. Not the most perceptive remark of his life, while his heart just kept on lifting like a hot-air balloon.

Tammy, Tammy, Tammy.

The tip of a chilli nudged the creamy slope of one breast

the way his tongue had nudged the same spot the other night. His breath caught for a moment in his chest when he thought about it, but then he saw that she hadn't smiled at him, still hadn't moved, and her face and lips were white.

And then she spoke.

'I—I—I can't do this,' she gasped. 'I can't bear it. I should have known.'

She fled before he could answer, turning and pushing through the crowd to disappear within seconds, while his thought processes moved like snails. She thought— Tarsha was standing there, dressed to the nines and dragging on his arm, and Tammy thought—

'That's her, isn't it?' Tarsha said quietly beside him, after the blood beating in his ears had begun to subside and understanding had dawned.

'Yes, and she thinks—'

'I could see what she thinks. What a royal mess we're all in today!'

'Oh, hell! Hell! She talked to me about it. The kind of woman I should be going out with. She thinks—'

'Aren't you going to go after her and set her straight? You look like death warmed up.'

He turned a stricken, unseeing look in Tarsha's direction. 'Would she believe me?'

Tarsha gave a tiny shrug, her mouth turned down, then said, 'If it's any consolation, *I* believe you. I never thought I'd see such a look on your face, Laird. Forget all the advice I gave you before about getting off lightly. You crazy man, I think you're really in love with her.'

'I know I am,' he said bleakly. 'I couldn't possibly feel like this if I wasn't. Lord, there's no more doubt, no thinking it through, I just am. I love her. Oh, hell. I *love* her.' He wanted to keep saying it, but he wasn't saying it to the right woman. 'Help me find her, Tarsh, so I can tell her and get this right for once.'

She touched his arm, way more in control than he was. 'We'll separate, and meet back at the marquee every half-hour.'

'Every half-*hour*?' He didn't want to have to wait five minutes to get that stricken, wounded look off Tammy's face, let alone half an hour or more.

'Laird, there's a huge crush of people here, and she's hurting so much. She doesn't want to be found. She has several minutes' head start on us already. I admit she stands out in a crowd, but how easy do you think this is going to be?'

Kelly and Liz would be worried.

It wasn't too hard to hide at the Melbourne Cup. There were so many people here. Tammy could easily have spent the whole day at Flemington Racecourse and never chanced to cross paths once with Laird and the gorgeous woman on his arm. She could have gone for weeks without knowing the truth, thinking there was still a chance, kidding herself that Laird staying away from her would make him realise how much he wanted to be with her. Permanently.

Fate had decreed otherwise.

'It's good that I saw them,' she mouthed to herself. 'It's good. It's for the best. It's over with, now. Short and sweet.'

But, oh, she didn't want to see them again!

She wanted to hide from Laird and his model, from Kelly and Liz, from the whole world and her own Laird-less future, and just lick her aching wounds. She found the quietest corner of the parade ring and stood there, watching the strappers walking their horses around before each race. She lined up at a drink kiosk for some iced water to cool her dry mouth. She hid out in front of the mirrors in several different ladies' rooms, soaking her handkerchief under the tap in order to press it to her tear-swollen eyes.

Which was where Laird's thin, gorgeous friend eventually found her and tried to tell her that she had it all wrong.

'Tammy, he and I are not involved. I promise. You must believe it. I've never seen him so distressed. You're the woman he wants. He's here with me today because I asked him to come with me as a favour, that's all.'

She explained about their past involvement, and the fact that she needed a man on her arm at important functions. She seemed genuine and sympathetic and urgent about all of it.

'I believe you,' Tammy said eventually. The strength had returned to her legs. Her chest no longer ached like a knife wound every time she breathed. Life could go on. 'But it doesn't make any real difference.' Because she knew it didn't.

'How can it not make a difference?' Laird's friend had begun to sound a little impatient by this point.

Her name was Tarsha. She seemed extremely nice, but she had the brittle, fast-paced confidence of a successful and sophisticated woman who didn't have time to sit around on Cup Day while a suburban mum cried on her shoulder. The ladies' room had begun to empty out…Tammy couldn't think why…and they had it almost to themselves, apart from a cleaning team filling the air with the pungent scents of disinfectant and lemon.

It was the most ludicrous place for a heart-to-heart, and yet somehow they were having one.

'Because there's always going to be a thin, single, gorgeous, socially appropriate woman,' Tammy said. 'Whether she's real, or a misunderstanding, like you turned out to be, or just my own stupid imagination, she's going to be there, somewhere, ready and waiting. She's the woman Laird should find to fall in love with, and I'll always know it, I'll always be waiting for it and it will always get in the way. If Laird and I... If by some miracle he did decide he was serious about me...'

'Tammy, he *is* serious about you.'

'I'd never be able to believe it with my whole heart. Some part of me would always be waiting for the thin, single, appropriate woman to show up and ruin my life.'

'He's had enough of those in the past. I know his mother. If he wanted a woman like that, he would have picked one by now.'

'A woman he could have his own children with, Tarsha. One who'd look as good on his arm as you do. One whose only baggage is her designer wardrobe.'

Tarsha fixed her with a critical eye. 'Tammy, you look damned fantastic in that ridiculous outfit, let me tell you. It's only women who think that women should be thin as rakes, not men. And can't he have his own children with you?'

'I—I...' She hadn't even considered it.

'I mean, have you had some gynae thing done, or something so you can't? Sorry to pry!'

'No, but—'

'You already have five, including triplets...'

'Oh, he's told you?'

'Trust me, he talks about you. And from what he's said, he's thoroughly enjoying your baggage.'

'Oh.'

'So would another couple of babies really make things so much harder? He has that property. Hobby farm, he always calls it now.'

'Does he?'

*That's because of me.*

Like the fact that he'd talked about her to Tarsha, the realisation gave Tammy a flicker of something she didn't dare to call hope.

'And he has enough money for fleets of help. Tell me.' Tarsha fixed her with gorgeous, impatient, dark-eyed scrutiny. 'Wouldn't you have a child with Laird, if he wanted one?'

'Yes, any time he said the word,' Tammy confessed, and flushed.

'As for the thin and gorgeous part...' She took a sweeping look over Tammy's generous figure and the bold chilli colours that mocked her emotional state of mind. 'He wants you, Tammy. Trust it.'

'I—I can't.'

Trust? After Tom? The very word scared her. Trust was only a code word for 'no safety net', and Tammy felt like a tightrope walker still only halfway across, with Niagara Falls gushing below. She hadn't had a safety net since Tom had left and she was just about managing, just about used to it, just about ready to think that as long as she had Mum and her own determined strength, a safety net wasn't required...

How could she dare to lose all that hard-won strength and self-reliance now?

She couldn't. The thought scared her too much.

'Well, I can't do any more to convince you,' Tarsha said. 'Except to say life can be short.' She sighed. 'If you see a chance at happiness, grab it before something happens. Don't wait, Tammy. Don't say no to it just because you're scared it might not always stay as rosy and beautiful as it is at first. And don't say no because you've been hurt. There's always the chance that life will hurt. Because none of us, even the luckiest and most blessed, ever know what's around the corner, do we?' She brushed something that might have been a crooked eyelash from the corner of one eye, and then blinked. She was...

'Tarsha, I'm sorry, are you...?' Crying.

'My make-up.'

It wasn't. She had tears in her eyes, and for the first time Tammy managed to look beyond her own turbulent emotions to discover that Tarsha had problems, too. 'What's wrong?'

'I'm fine.'

'You're not.'

'Really. We're just about to miss the big race.'

'Do you care about the big race?' Tammy asked gently.

'No, not in the slightest.'

'And you've just wangled my darkest emotional secrets out of me when we don't even know each other. Couldn't I return the favour?'

'Where do you want me to start?' Tarsha asked. 'With the man in Europe who's just left his wife, but doesn't know how I feel about him? Or the new modelling agency I don't know if I can manage to get off the ground? Or the—?' She stopped. Looked at Tammy. Narrowed her eyes. Pressed her lips together, then opened them again. 'You're a nurse,' she said.

'Yes.'

'You know about this stuff.' She brushed her fingers across the underside of her left breast and grimaced. 'I haven't told Laird. I don't know if it's my imagination, or if it means anything. Tammy, I—I— Why the hell am I telling you? I've got to tell someone. I felt a lump in my breast in the shower this morning.'

# CHAPTER ELEVEN

LAIRD had lost Tarsha, now, too.

She'd missed the past two rendezvous they'd scheduled at L'Occidentale's marquee, and he couldn't see her anywhere in the crowd. Somehow, she just didn't stand out the way Tammy did. Race 6 had been run and the winner had been paraded in all his sleek and rug-bedecked glory before the crowd. Twenty-four horses were now being loaded into the barriers for the Cup itself.

And Laird didn't remotely care.

He pushed through the crush of people, scanning the bobbing hats for the only one at the whole of Flemington Racecourse that was covered in red plastic chillies, cursing his own impatience, Tarsha's unpunctuality and the fact that he'd ever agreed to the role of escort in the first place.

The race caller began reeling out the details of the race. The horses were off and running. A string of early leaders gave way to new hopes. One lacklustre performer could 'see them all' five lengths in the rear. The crowd's focus was noisy and electric, but surely Tammy and Tarsha weren't among all those people watching the track when they knew he was looking for them. He realised he was searching in the wrong place.

Away from the course, scanning for them was easier. He caught sight of Tarsha at last, after only a couple of minutes, and even though Tammy wasn't with her, he hurried up to her in a rush of relief. 'Where have you been? Did you find her? You must have, surely!'

'I did.'

'So where is she now? Why isn't she with you?' He had to raise his voice to be heard, because the amplified race commentary had reached fever pitch, the sound booming and distorted and the caller not even pausing for breath. The horses were into the final straight and almost at the finish.

'She's gone back to her friends.'

'But I wanted—'

Tarsha laid a hand on his arm. 'Don't you want to see who wins?'

'No, damn it!' It was over anyway. Some people cheered and hugged and laughed. Others tore up their betting slips with expressions of disgust. Laird had no clue about any of the placings, and cared even less. He was distantly aware that Tarsha looked exhausted, although she was trying to hide it. Probably the shoes pinching her feet. 'Tell me about Tammy!'

'She's lovely, somewhat to my surprise,' Tarsha said. 'You do have some taste in women after all. We had a really good talk.'

'Where? Where the hell did you go that I couldn't find you and you took so long?'

'In the ladies' room. Sorry. Unintentionally inaccessible, as far as you're concerned.' She turned down her mouth. 'Turned out we had a lot of ground to cover.'

'So tell me what she said.'

Tarsha sighed. 'She's strong, Laird, but very vulnerable. If you ever hurt—'

'Don't you dare tell me not to hurt her!' he exploded. 'I don't have the remotest intention of hurting her.'

'The problem is, I'm not sure how you're ever going to get her to believe that…'

She outlined what Tammy had said. And Laird's understanding of how he felt about her and his frustration at not being able to find either her or Tarsha for two hours, along with the crowd-borne atmosphere of let-down now that the race was over, coalesced into a sensation of hopelessness that made him feel ill and almost paralysed.

'Then it's a lost cause,' he said bleakly. 'She wanted me to take time to think, but she's done some thinking of her own, and this is what she's come up with. And you're right, I don't know how to convince her. Words aren't enough. I can't think of anything that would be enough, if what you've said is true. Thin, single and gorgeous. Oh, hell!'

Tarsha touched his shoulder. 'Hey, is this the Laird Burchell I know? The one who never had time to go out with me twelve years ago because coming a mere second in his exams wasn't good enough? The one who turns babies into miracles every week? We're not giving up on this without a fight.'

'Tarsha—'

'I've never seen you in such a mess. That means something. That tells me we have to take action.'

'Does it?'

She did that tired, odd, upside-down smile again. 'As a wise woman in a very strange hat said to me only recently, Laird...you're not dead yet.'

'You didn't have to come with me. Go, if you need to. You must have...nappies to buy, or something.'

'Four-year-olds aren't still in nappies.'

Tarsha was unfamiliar with the finer details of child-rearing, and she was horribly, painfully, desperately nervous. Waiting for a fine-needle aspiration in the outpatients department at Yarra Hospital on Thursday morning, she sat beside Tammy with her knees locked tight together and her hands folded even tighter in her lap. The tart wit and tight pose were a poised ex-model's version of falling completely apart, Tammy realised.

'Of course I had to come with you,' she told Tarsha, feeling an odd degree of protectiveness towards a woman facing the possibility of cancer whom she hadn't even met this time two days ago. 'You needed someone here. And since you're stubbornly refusing to tell anyone else about this...'

'Oh, please,' Tarsha drawled. 'As if stubbornness isn't your middle name, too.'

They were running late that morning in Outpatients, and Tarsha had used the window of unexpected time as an opportunity to bring up the subject of Laird. Until Tammy had—shaky-voiced—begged her to stop. 'It's myself I doubt, Tarsha, far more than I doubt him.'

'Has he phoned you since Tuesday?'

'Three times.'

'What did you say to him?'

'No.' To everything. To the dinner invitation. To the plea to talk. To the proposal of marriage, made in a moment of sheer frustration and accompanied by swearing. *If I asked you to marry me right now, over the phone, damn it, would that make a difference?* 'I said no...'

'Have you seen him at work?'

'No, but I will this afternoon.'

'Good! I hope it's really uncomfortable for you!'

'Thanks,' Tammy smiled a little crookedly. 'I like you, too, Tarsha.'

'I'm too bloody terrified to be tactful right now. As for being stubborn, I'm just really good at believing that if you don't talk about something it isn't happening. And that, if the *something* is medical, talking about it to a nurse doesn't count!'

'Similar theory to the one that says that ice cream eaten while standing in front of the fridge doesn't have any calories.'

'There are some really good theories around these days, aren't there?' She gave a breathy, wobbly laugh.

'There are, indeed. And there probably is nothing happening, Tarsha. If the ultrasound and manual exam had set off major alarm bells, they would have gone straight to a surgical biopsy.'

'I did tell one other person...' Tarsha said slowly.

'Not Laird.'

'No, not Laird. Someone in Europe. He says he's coming out here to see me as soon as he can. That would be the best news in the world, if I didn't have this hanging over me. As it is, I'm too scared to be happy, which feels—' She broke off and changed tack. 'Thanks, Tammy. For coming. For saying the right things.'

'It's fine.'

'For putting up with me nagging you about Laird. Because I do suddenly understand how a woman can feel too scared to be happy, even when a man says he cares. I give you fair warning, though, I'm already planning how I'm going to pay you back for your time!'

'I'm scared about that now...'

'You wait,' Tarsha threatened lightly, then her voice changed. 'Tell me again why this is much better than a surgical biopsy, where I'd be nicely asleep and wouldn't know it was happening.'

'Because there's very little risk of anything going wrong—infection or scarring. The needle is so fine, Tarsha, it should be no worse than a blood test. It'll be over within a few minutes, and you'll have the result in a couple of days. Do you want me to come in with you?'

'No, because then you'll see what a wimp I am.'

'I can already see what a wimp you are.'

'Oh, hell, I thought I was hiding it really well!'

At that moment, the doctor came out and called Tarsha's name.

On Thursday afternoon, Laird judged that baby Adam was ready to be extubated from the ventilator and put back onto CPAP. He'd responded well to treatment over the past three days, and his bowels and kidneys were both showing signs of better function.

Tammy arrived at one o'clock for an afternoon shift, and even though it was hardly a surprise to Laird to see her here, the way it had been two days ago at Flemington Racecourse, his reaction was the same—instinctive pleasure that made him feel almost giddy, coupled with a gut-level sense of hopelessness and frustration.

He and Tarsha had limped through the rest of their day at the races with conversation kept to superficial subjects. As much as he had, she'd had something on her mind, only she'd refused to talk about it. And on the subject of Tammy, there hadn't been anything more to say.

He'd offered to find Tarsha more champagne and she'd said no. She'd clapped her hands when his chosen horse, backed for more than he usually put on, had placed second in the final race. 'Fantastic, Laird! That's three hundred dollars!'

But she hadn't really been *there*.

If it had been Tammy holding him at such a preoccupied distance he'd have confronted her over it.

*What's wrong? Let's talk about this.*

He'd have held her by the shoulders and demanded answers from her and he knew she would have given them. He might have ended up angry with her, the way he'd been angry a few weeks ago when she'd kept refusing his coffee and dinner invitations—a torrid, undisciplined, demanding kind of anger that he'd barely recognised in himself then, but which seemed far more familiar now. He'd experienced it three times since Tuesday, over the phone.

There was no comparison between Tarsha and Tammy in his heart, only he didn't yet know how he could get her to believe that.

The sight of her working beside baby Adam's humidicrib

sent every system in his body into overload. She was giving the little boy a dose of medication—a form of caffeine to keep him alert enough to prevent apnoea episodes, ready for his shift from the ventilator to the CPAP machine.

She had one of those unflattering caps on, as usual, but somehow she still looked beautiful. Or not even that. It was irrelevant to him now whether she was beautiful or not. Irrelevant what any other man would think. His whole body simply said, *That's her! That's the woman I love!* and responded accordingly, with a sense of recognition and happiness and painful physical wanting and just…rightness. Pure, simple rightness, which was the most convincing indicator of all.

It was a rightness Tammy didn't trust, according to Tarsha. 'Laird, you'll just have to convince her! Give it time!'

Glancing at him and then quickly away, Tammy gave an awkward greeting, then said, 'He's ready, Dr Burchell. I have everything on hand.'

There were too many people around, the usual unavoidable crowds in the NICU—parents and staff, desperately trying to stay quiet and calm and not get in each other's way or bump into equipment and trolleys and baby cots. All the same, Laird dropped his voice and said to her, 'When's your break? Can we talk?'

'We already have. On the phone.'

'Look at me, Tammy.'

He could see she didn't want to—that she didn't dare, because she knew how much her face would tell him. Her eyes lifted reluctantly. Her cheeks had flushed and her pupils were big and dark.

'What's it going to take, Tammy?'

'I don't know. We can't talk about it now. No, no.' She raised a hand, warning him off. 'We don't need to talk about it at all. We have talked about it. And I know you're going to try flowers and chocolates and wine and lovely words and promises. I'm more scared of those things than of anything else.'

'Because you're scared they'll convince you,' he said, with a flare of satisfaction.

'And then they won't last.'

'Right, standing order from the florist and a few wineries for the next forty years, that's easy...'

She laughed, even though she didn't want to. 'Don't. We have a baby to take care of.'

'All right, you win.' He added threateningly, 'For now.'

The procedure wasn't long or difficult, and soon Adam had the nasal prongs attached and the oxygen flowing. The rate and pressure could be changed in response to his oxygen saturation levels, if needed.

'I really hope he doesn't have any more setbacks,' Tammy murmured. 'Those kidneys still aren't great, are they?'

'Improving.'

'Not enough.'

'He's on bicarbonate of soda now, to correct his acid balance.'

'Yes, I saw that in his notes,' she said. 'We just need to get him bigger and stronger, get that TPN line out and those creatinine levels down. He's changed over the past few days. I think he's fighting harder.'

'So am I, Tammy Prunty,' he warned her. 'So am I.'

\* \* \*

Tammy finished her shift at three o'clock on Friday afternoon. She wasn't due to work again until Tuesday night, thanks to some juggling of hours that another nurse had asked for. It was a longer break than usual, the longest she'd taken since she'd started working here at Yarra Hospital, and she knew she should consider it well timed.

Four days without seeing Laird.

Four days without seeing any of these babies either.

Both prospects unsettled her. In the NICU, a lot could change in four days.

Despite the usual need to hurry home to give Mum some help with five kids who would be tired at the end of the school week, she found herself lingering. 'See you next week, Alison. Hope you get some more cuddles with him on the weekend.'

'Before you go, Tammy,' Fran said. She had fragile little Adam in her arms. 'Could you take a picture or two? Do you have a minute to spare? I remembered to bring the camera in today, and now I'm almost forgetting to use it.'

So Tammy stayed and took some pictures, and Alison said, 'One day, Fran, you won't be able to believe he was ever this small.'

'So I'm told…' She sighed, unable to come up with the imagination and faith that Adam would ever be bigger. And maybe, if the worst happened, he wouldn't. His mother was thinking about it. 'Whatever happens, we'll have the photos,' she whispered. 'And I'll be able to remember how it felt to hold him.'

Click, click, click went the camera. Tammy took a couple of Alison and her baby as well. Alison and Fran were good friends now, and intended to keep in touch after the beckoning, elusive day when their time in the NICU would end. She paused for one more look at the two mothers, wondering what she'd see in their faces next week when she came in.

'Do we have a bed?' Tammy heard one of the nurses at the desk asking as she passed by on her way out. 'Royal Victoria wants to send us a mum in pre-term labour. Twenty-six weeks so there'll be a baby coming in here.'

New babies, and babies leaving. Endings and beginnings. Tragedy and joy. Nothing stayed the same for long. Tammy had an odd feeling as she left the unit and took the lift. As if she was saying goodbye to something, only she didn't know what it was.

She found Tarsha waiting for her in front of the gift shop on the ground floor. She was smiling, her eyes were bright, and she had just one word to say. 'Benign!'

'Tarsha, that's wonderful!' They hugged each other, laughing.

Tarsha had her car keys in her hand. 'So we're celebrating.'

'Oh, lord, I'm sorry, but I can't! I have to get home to the kids.'

'You don't. I've arranged it. A professional nanny to help your mother, and she knows all about it.'

'A nanny? For how long? Tarsha, you didn't have to—'

'Trust me, I had to. May I say that wonderful word again? *Benign.* Isn't it beautiful? I'm kidnapping you, Tammy, accept it now. When you walk back into that NICU of yours next week, you won't be the same person.'

'Because benign is such a beautiful word?'

'Because I told you I'd pay you back for your time, and I am.'

Somehow Tammy was expecting a spa massage or a salon facial.

She wasn't expecting Laird. It wasn't until she began to recognise the route out to the vineyard—and she suspected that Tarsha had taken a few unnecessary turnings and side streets to disguise their destination for longer—that she realised where they were going.

'No! Take me home. I want my car! This is your idea of how to pay me back for coming to the doctor with you?'

'Idea?' Tarsha's eyes didn't leave the road. Her smile was wicked and creamy. 'It's way more than an idea, Tammy. It's a major conspiracy.'

'Then Laird's in on it...'

'And so is your mother.'

'So the nanny is supposed to be—'

'Staying till bedtime.'

And Tammy was supposed to be staying at the vineyard all night.


Laird looked visibly on edge when Tammy caught sight of him. He was standing in his front yard, beside the steps leading up to the house, his eyes fixed on the approach of Tarsha's car. With the afternoon sun shining in her face, Tammy guessed that the windscreen must be reflecting the light too brightly for Laird to see inside.

*He doesn't know if Tarsha managed to get me here, and he'll be gutted if she didn't.*

Her stomach lurched at the thought that she was this important to him, that he was this certain about how he felt, that she had the power to hurt him the same way he had the power to hurt her. She trusted that neither of them would ever use it deliberately, and yet...

Give in, said a huge part of her. Let yourself feel it, too. You want to.

In so many ways, it would be so easy.

He'd seen her. She saw his sudden grin, the energy that shot through his strong body, and her stomach flipped again. The strength drained out of her legs, and Tarsha had the driver's side door open and was out of the car while Tammy was still struggling to move.

'I'm very good at this, Laird. She didn't suspect a thing.'

'You made darned sure I didn't, Tarsha,' Tammy said weakly. Laird was still grinning.

But Tarsha had clicked open the car boot, and had her head hidden inside. 'Here's your overnight gear, Tammy. Your mother packed it, so you'll have to blame her if she forgot your toothbrush.' She put the bag into Tammy's boneless hands and climbed back into the driver's seat.

'Wait...!'

'Absolutely not! I have someone to meet off his international flight at the airport first thing tomorrow morning, and I have shopping to do.'

'Who is she meeting?' Tammy asked, slow on the uptake, as Tarsha drove away.

'His name is Olivier,' Laird said.

'The man in Europe. He's really coming, and she didn't tell me!'

'I think she still doesn't dare to believe it'll work out the way she wants.' They looked at each other, and there was a frozen moment in which all Tammy could feel was the beating of her heart. 'I don't dare to believe it with you either,' Laird added in a low voice. 'Can you put me out of my misery, Tammy?'

'No…' But she probably hadn't managed to hide how much she wanted to say yes.

'Oh, hell! I'm not going to accept it!'

'No…well, that's nice. Flattering.'

'It's not flattering! It's just a fact. And it's going to be a damned nuisance for you, I'm warning you now!'

'I—I know.' Her heart flipped, making her feel giddy and happy and scared all at the same time.

'Let's go for a walk. I can't take you into the house. I won't be able to keep my hands off you. Which is idiotic, because the house is where I have all my best seduction techniques ready to go.'

'Seduction techniques, Laird?'

'Champagne chilling, music playing, something fantastic involving chicken and sour cream and white wine slow-cooking in the oven, purely to prove I can cook if I have to. And here I am denying us both the opportunity to impress you, because if that's not what you bloody want…'

He gritted his teeth and sighed, and she reached out and slid her arm through his, unable to speak. They began to walk, aimless and barely noticing where their feet led.

'I can't force you, Tammy,' he said. 'I can't even mount a strenuous argument. I…' He shook his head. 'I don't have anything else to offer than what I've offered already. My heart and my faith. And if those things aren't enough, I'm not going to beat you over the head with them. But I'm not going to let you go either.'

The paddocks and the vines were green and glowing in the afternoon sun. In the distance horses grazed, and in the paddock closest to the house were the two ponies and Solly the donkey. Laird and Tammy stopped by the fence and looked at them, not knowing what to say to each other, not knowing where to go next.

The animals came closer, hoping for treats. Banana put his nose over the fence and nuzzled at the pocket of Laird's jeans. 'Sorry, boy, no carrots or apples today,' he said. Then he went still—so dramatically still, with his hand poised on a fencepost and an odd light in his eyes, that Tammy's heart started to beat faster.

'What's wrong, Laird?'

'People even choke on apples,' he said.

'Sometimes…But—'

'Don't you remember? That's what you said last weekend when we had the girls here and Sarah wanted to trot. We were talking about risks, about nothing in life having a guarantee of safety, and you said that people can even choke on apples. They're delicious and good for you, but very occasionally people choke on them. And it was such a wonderful Tammy-ish thing to say. Because it's true. And it's so simple. Such a simple rule about how to live your life, in a spirit of faith but with your eyes wide open at the same time.'

He turned to her with his face lit up, as if he'd found the answer. Maybe he had.

'So simple, Tammy,' he murmured, 'and yet you won't believe in it yourself, even now, when it's so important.'

He wrapped his arms around her and buried his face in the curve of her neck. Not close enough. She wanted his mouth on hers, so she shamelessly sought it out and kissed him, tears on her lashes, dizzy with love and fear. Was there a chance that love was going to win?

'Be with me,' he whispered. 'Love me. Take the risk. We'll take it together. It's that simple.'

'How can it be?'

'It can be. It just is.' He kissed her again, and she couldn't hide the sweet weakness in her legs or the way she wanted to hold him and lean her head against his heart. As usual, she was betraying everything to him, and she didn't care.

'Oh, Laird…'

'I love you,' he said. 'I know it's too soon to say any of this, and I don't care. I know there's a lot to work out, and I don't care about that either. All I know is that I've never felt like this before, and love is the only word that fits, and everything else follows from there. Trust. Faith. It has to follow. It's like the sun rising in the morning. Because you love me, too.'

'You're not even asking me, are you?'

'No, now I'm telling you. I'm *ordering* you. I'm not messing around, and I'm not taking no for an answer. You love me. Repeat after me, "I love you, Laird."'

'I love you, Laird,' she said helplessly.

'There. Was that so hard?'

'That's the easy part.'

'It's the powerful part. It's the engine that drives everything else. We're not going to rush this. We're not going to skimp on the details. But we're going to get there.'

'Where's there? What's happening then?'

'You're going to marry me,' he predicted, with a medical specialist's arrogant certainty, and the same blunt honesty that she'd delivered to him from the start. 'When the time is right, I'm going to ask you, with bells and whistles and my whole heart on a plate, and you're going to say yes, the moment I do.'

\* \* \*

She did say yes.

Six months later.

After they'd spent many mornings at the garden centre, buying way too many shrubs and trees, and three weekends at the beach, making castles in the sand. After they'd taken all five kids on countless pony rides at the vineyard—with a few more falls and lots of carrots and apples. After they'd spent some time getting to know each other's parents, and taken evenings out for just the two of them, tasting from each other's plates.

He asked her to marry him at the vineyard in the autumn on a mellow, golden afternoon, and they had the wedding there, too, several months later, with Laura, Lucy and Sarah as flower girls and Lachlan and Ben firmly declining any formal role. Tammy wore a cream dress of soft lace that hugged the figure Laird found so luscious and wonderful, and Laird wore a suit that was quite definitely Armani this time, thanks very much.

It was a September wedding, out of doors on the back lawn, edged by the new roses, with Amira, Banana and Solly looking on. Oh, and several ducks, too. The weather had begun to warm up and the new pale green growth had begun to appear on the vines. Tarsha was there, with Olivier. They had wedding plans of their own, but she was driving her fiancé mad with her quest for the right designer to make her dress. They had been travelling back and forth between Australia and Europe for several months, sorting out their lives.

The details of Tammy and Laird's new life were already in place. Tammy was selling her house in the suburbs and she and Mum and the children were moving out to the vineyard. There was a little cottage on the corner of the property, which Mum had already begun to make her own. Laird was keeping his townhouse near the hospital for times when the forty-five-minute drive between the hospital and the vineyard seemed too far for a busy neonatal specialist and his wife.

Tammy expected that she would be cajoled into taking frequent second honeymoons in the townhouse with her new husband. She'd already told her mother, 'It's too much for you, Mum.'

But Mum hadn't listened. 'You're cutting down to two shifts a week at the hospital. Of course I can look after the kids while you spend some time on your own with Laird. He doesn't want to have to come home from the hospital to an empty place in town on the nights he doesn't drive out here. And you're getting professional help with the house. The kids and I will have a ball with the ducks and the donkey and the ponies on our own, when you two aren't around.'

Tammy suspected that hand-reared lambs were only a breeding season away.

And maybe another kind of hand-reared infant as well. The human kind. There was plenty of room in their lives for six ducks, a donkey, two ponies, two lambs, five children and a baby.

And yet somehow, despite all of this, as Laird had said, it was very simple, like the goodness of apples.

They loved each other, which made everything else fall into place.

### MILLS & BOON®
*Pure reading pleasure*

# JUNE 2008 HARDBACK TITLES

## ROMANCE

| | |
|---|---|
| **Hired: The Sheikh's Secretary Mistress** *Lucy Monroe* | 978 0 263 20302 8 |
| **The Billionaire's Blackmailed Bride** *Jacqueline Baird* | 978 0 263 20303 5 |
| **The Sicilian's Innocent Mistress** *Carole Mortimer* | 978 0 263 20304 2 |
| **The Sheikh's Defiant Bride** *Sandra Marton* | 978 0 263 20305 9 |
| **Italian Boss, Ruthless Revenge** *Carol Marinelli* | 978 0 263 20306 6 |
| **The Mediterranean Prince's Captive Virgin** *Robyn Donald* | 978 0 263 20307 3 |
| **Mistress: Hired for the Billionaire's Pleasure** *India Grey* | 978 0 263 20308 0 |
| **The Italian's Unwilling Wife** *Kathryn Ross* | 978 0 263 20309 7 |
| **Wanted: Royal Wife and Mother** *Marion Lennox* | 978 0 263 20310 3 |
| **The Boss's Unconventional Assistant** *Jennie Adams* | 978 0 263 20311 0 |
| **Inherited: Instant Family** *Judy Christenberry* | 978 0 263 20312 7 |
| **The Prince's Secret Bride** *Raye Morgan* | 978 0 263 20313 4 |
| **Milllionaire Dad, Nanny Needed!** *Susan Meier* | 978 0 263 20314 1 |
| **Falling for Mr Dark & Dangerous** *Donna Alward* | 978 0 263 20315 8 |
| **The Spanish Doctor's Love-Child** *Kate Hardy* | 978 0 263 20316 5 |
| **Her Very Special Boss** *Anne Fraser* | 978 0 263 20317 2 |

## HISTORICAL

| | |
|---|---|
| **Miss Winthorpe's Elopement** *Christine Merrill* | 978 0 263 20201 4 |
| **The Rake's Unconventional Mistress** *Juliet Landon* | 978 0 263 20202 1 |
| **Rags-to-Riches Bride** *Mary Nichols* | 978 0 263 20203 8 |

## MEDICAL™

| | |
|---|---|
| **Their Miracle Baby** *Caroline Anderson* | 978 0 263 19898 0 |
| **The Children's Doctor and the Single Mum** *Lilian Darcy* | 978 0 263 19899 7 |
| **Pregnant Nurse, New-Found Family** *Lynne Marshall* | 978 0 263 19900 0 |
| **The GP's Marriage Wish** *Judy Campbell* | 978 0 263 19901 7 |

MILLS & BOON®
*Pure reading pleasure*

0508 Gen Std LP

# JUNE 2008 LARGE PRINT TITLES

## ROMANCE

| | |
|---|---|
| **The Greek Tycoon's Defiant Bride** *Lynne Graham* | 978 0 263 20050 8 |
| **The Italian's Rags-to-Riches Wife** *Julia James* | 978 0 263 20051 5 |
| **Taken by Her Greek Boss** *Cathy Williams* | 978 0 263 20052 2 |
| **Bedded for the Italian's Pleasure** *Anne Mather* | 978 0 263 20053 9 |
| **Cattle Rancher, Secret Son** *Margaret Way* | 978 0 263 20054 6 |
| **Rescued by the Sheikh** *Barbara McMahon* | 978 0 263 20055 3 |
| **Her One and Only Valentine** *Trish Wylie* | 978 0 263 20056 0 |
| **English Lord, Ordinary Lady** *Fiona Harper* | 978 0 263 20057 7 |

## HISTORICAL

| | |
|---|---|
| **A Compromised Lady** *Elizabeth Rolls* | 978 0 263 20157 4 |
| **Runaway Miss** *Mary Nichols* | 978 0 263 20158 1 |
| **My Lady Innocent** *Annie Burrows* | 978 0 263 20159 8 |

## MEDICAL™

| | |
|---|---|
| **Christmas Eve Baby** *Caroline Anderson* | 978 0 263 19956 7 |
| **Long-Lost Son: Brand New Family** *Lilian Darcy* | 978 0 263 19957 4 |
| **Their Little Christmas Miracle** *Jennifer Taylor* | 978 0 263 19958 1 |
| **Twins for a Christmas Bride** *Josie Metcalfe* | 978 0 263 19959 8 |
| **The Doctor's Very Special Christmas** *Kate Hardy* | 978 0 263 19960 4 |
| **A Pregnant Nurse's Christmas Wish** *Meredith Webber* | 978 0 263 19961 1 |

# JULY 2008 HARDBACK TITLES

## ROMANCE

| | |
|---|---|
| **The De Santis Marriage** *Michelle Reid* | 978 0 263 20318 9 |
| **Greek Tycoon, Waitress Wife** *Julia James* | 978 0 263 20319 6 |
| **The Italian Boss's Mistress of Revenge** *Trish Morey* | 978 0 263 20320 2 |
| **One Night with His Virgin Mistress** *Sara Craven* | 978 0 263 20321 9 |
| **Bedded by the Greek Billionaire** *Kate Walker* | 978 0 263 20322 6 |
| **Secretary Mistress, Convenient Wife** *Maggie Cox* | 978 0 263 20323 3 |
| **The Billionaire's Blackmail Bargain** *Margaret Mayo* | 978 0 263 20324 0 |
| **The Italian's Bought Bride** *Kate Hewitt* | 978 0 263 20325 7 |
| **Wedding at Wangaree Valley** *Margaret Way* | 978 0 263 20326 4 |
| **Crazy about her Spanish Boss** *Rebecca Winters* | 978 0 263 20327 1 |
| **The Millionaire's Proposal** *Trish Wylie* | 978 0 263 20328 8 |
| **Abby and the Playboy Prince** *Raye Morgan* | 978 0 263 20329 5 |
| **The Bridegroom's Secret** *Melissa James* | 978 0 263 20330 1 |
| **Texas Ranger Takes a Bride** *Patricia Thayer* | 978 0 263 20331 8 |
| **A Doctor, A Nurse: A Little Miracle** *Carol Marinelli* | 978 0 263 20332 5 |
| **The Playboy Doctor's Marriage Proposal** *Fiona Lowe* | 978 0 263 20333 2 |

## HISTORICAL

| | |
|---|---|
| **The Shocking Lord Standon** *Louise Allen* | 978 0 263 20204 5 |
| **His Cavalry Lady** *Joanna Maitland* | 978 0 263 20205 2 |
| **An Honourable Rogue** *Carol Townend* | 978 0 263 20206 9 |

## MEDICAL™

| | |
|---|---|
| **Sheikh Surgeon Claims His Bride** *Josie Metcalfe* | 978 0 263 19902 4 |
| **A Proposal Worth Waiting For** *Lilian Darcy* | 978 0 263 19903 1 |
| **Top-Notch Surgeon, Pregnant Nurse** *Amy Andrews* | 978 0 263 19904 8 |
| **A Mother for His Son** *Gill Sanderson* | 978 0 263 19905 5 |

# JULY 2008 LARGE PRINT TITLES

## ROMANCE

| | |
|---|---|
| **The Martinez Marriage Revenge** *Helen Bianchin* | 978 0 263 20058 4 |
| **The Sheikh's Convenient Virgin** *Trish Morey* | 978 0 263 20059 1 |
| **King of the Desert, Captive Bride** *Jane Porter* | 978 0 263 20060 7 |
| **Spanish Billionaire, Innocent Wife** *Kate Walker* | 978 0 263 20061 4 |
| **A Royal Marriage of Convenience** <br> *Marion Lennox* | 978 0 263 20062 1 |
| **The Italian Tycoon and the Nanny** <br> *Rebecca Winters* | 978 0 263 20063 8 |
| **Promoted: to Wife and Mother** *Jessica Hart* | 978 0 263 20064 5 |
| **Falling for the Rebel Heir** *Ally Blake* | 978 0 263 20065 2 |

## HISTORICAL

| | |
|---|---|
| **The Dangerous Mr Ryder** *Louise Allen* | 978 0 263 20160 4 |
| **An Improper Aristocrat** *Deb Marlowe* | 978 0 263 20161 1 |
| **The Novice Bride** *Carol Townend* | 978 0 263 20162 8 |

## MEDICAL™

| | |
|---|---|
| **The Italian's New-Year Marriage Wish** <br> *Sarah Morgan* | 978 0 263 19962 8 |
| **The Doctor's Longed-For Family** *Joanna Neil* | 978 0 263 19963 5 |
| **Their Special-Care Baby** *Fiona McArthur* | 978 0 263 19964 2 |
| **Their Miracle Child** *Gill Sanderson* | 978 0 263 19965 9 |
| **Single Dad, Nurse Bride** *Lynne Marshall* | 978 0 263 19966 6 |
| **A Family for the Children's Doctor** <br> *Dianne Drake* | 978 0 263 19967 3 |